S. Howard-Taylor

Kate Byrne - A Novel

Vol. I

S. Howard-Taylor

Kate Byrne - A Novel
Vol. I

ISBN/EAN: 9783337031688

Printed in Europe, USA, Canada, Australia, Japan

Cover: Foto ©Andreas Hilbeck / pixelio.de

More available books at **www.hansebooks.com**

KATE BYRNE.

A Novel.

S. HOWARD-TAYLOR.

IN TWO VOLUMES.
VOL. I.

London:
SAMUEL TINSLEY,
10, SOUTHAMPTON STREET, STRAND.
1874.

KATE BYRNE.

CHAPTER I.

BOUT half-a-mile from one of the prettiest villages in Sellshire, and not very far from the county town, is a large, old-fashioned house, surrounded by a goodly number of fine trees. The grounds are very tastefully laid out; a thick hedge hid them and the house from the view of passers by in the late spring and summer; but when the shrubs and trees had not their full clothing on, as it were, which is the case when this story opens, any one on the high road could have seen a young girl flitting here and there in the bright morning sunshine of early Spring.

She was dividing her attention between the small fresh flowers and a large Newfoundland dog, whose frantic elephantine endeavours to come in for his full share of his mistress's favour were not quite as enjoyable to her as he may have imagined.

"Down, Rover; down, sir; you are too bad for anything!" she exclaimed. "I can scarcely stand against such force."

She held up a small whip, which she professed to carry for the express purpose of keeping Rover in order, but it seldom or ever fell heavily enough to make much impression on the aforesaid animal. She made a pretty picture as she stood there in her soft morning-gown, which hung in graceful folds about her neat little figure, a large straw hat shading her delicate complexion. She is about nineteen years of age, has large blue eyes, tiny hands

and feet, and a good deal of light, fine
hair. She is the only daughter of the
owner of the house, a widow lady, Mrs.
Leigh, and the best child in all the world,
her mother often said. Her father had
made a considerable fortune as a cotton-
merchant, and retired from business sooner
than most men are able to do now-a-days.
He purchased their present home, away
from all the bustle and toil of the city,
where he had lived all his life; but an
unfortunate speculation, in which he had
risked and lost some thousands, happened
soon after they had settled in their new
home, and this so preyed upon him, that
he got into a low, morbid state of health
and mind, and died of fever, leaving his
wife and daughter to mourn his loss. They
were, however, still in very good circumstances: there had been no real need for
poor Mr. Leigh to fall into despair and fear
ruin.

Mrs. Leigh was of a very good family,—
" gentle people," or what is more commonly
known as " county" people, who prided
themselves, to 'a great extent, upon their
good blood and breeding; so that when
their daughter resolved to marry a poor
man (as he was in those days, who began
life as an errand-boy, and was not ashamed
to mention it), their indignation certainly
knew no bounds. They could not, nor
would not, find the slightest excuse for her
so far forgetting what was due to the "blue
blood of the Harleys," for insulting them
and degrading herself, for exchanging their
refined poverty for the coarser companion-
ship of a man who they protested would
make her rue the step she was taking in a
single month. So she left her home under
the most trying circumstances, with no good
wishes or blessings attending her from those
she left behind. But dame Fortune, or Fate,
or some other dame equally variable and

capricious, decreed that Mrs. Leigh should not be so unutterably miserable and dejected as her friends had prophesied; on the contrary, all went well with her from the first. Her husband prospered in almost all his undertakings for many years, and was soon enabled, as we have seen, to carry out his one pet scheme of placing his stately, elegant wife, of whom he had always been so justly proud, in a position equal, at all events, in the more substantial senses and enjoyments, to the one from which he had taken her.

The Harleys allowed themselves, in due time, to be soothed and pacified, and unbent, so far as to allow themselves to visit " poor Mary" and "that man," as they always so sweetly called Mr. Leigh. They managed to make great use of his generous hospitality, were not too proud or too dignified to ride in his carriages and share his well-supplied table; but they no doubt looked upon him as the one benefited by the intimacy, and comforted themselves with the assurance that they were doing much more for him by visiting them than he ever could have expected. After his death they felt they had nothing to reproach themselves with. Mrs. Leigh was, of course, very glad to have them sometimes with her, she had so few relations, and only one child left. Of course she had felt their unkind treatment of her husband, but it was quite useless to show any resentment after he was gone, especially as they had, at least, appeared friendly for some time, and she well knew that he had never thought ill of them. Helen was placed at a good school in London till she had turned seventeen; she then went home to share her mother's quiet country life, and entered into all the duties which fell to her with great good-will and readiness. The village was large, and there was plenty of work for willing hands to do, as their vicar, Mr. Clayton, said to Helen; and he gladly accepted her young, active head and hands to help him in the parish and schools.

Her life at a fashionable London school had not made her too fine a lady, or given her any of those absurd, foolish ideas that so many young people have as to this or that not being fit for a lady to do. "The more we can help others the better, for surely time usefully employed can never be thrown away," Mrs. Leigh had said to her when a child. "And if there is no one in your own sphere to require your attention, there are plenty of your less fortunate fellow-creatures who will be truly glad of your help and consideration, which will cost you so little, my child, and be of great help to them." How much more real, lasting good might be done, especially around our country houses, where so many of the daughters of the wealthy pass most of their young days, if mothers would take care to impress upon them the advantage of finding out, by their own exertions, those among the poor who are really deserving; then those who are kindly disposed and anxious to do good would be less often imposed upon, and the needy and suffering greatly benefited.

The day before we introduced Mrs. Leigh and her daughter to the reader's notice, the former had had a long consultation with her lawyer, who had come from the North to see her on business matters. Some property she was anxious to dispose of had been all but purchased by another client of his, and as he had just then a little spare time, he had come to talk over final arrangements with her.

"Helen, my dear, Mr. Benson will dine with us to-day, and the Clennings are coming to meet him; but he will be back some time before dinner, as we have not quite finished with money matters. You need not go away though unless you like, love," said Mrs. Leigh.

"Oh, thank you, mamma. I hope you will excuse me till dinner. I dislike money matters so much,—and lawyers too, for that matter," she added, smiling,—"that until I am really obliged, I would rather have nothing to do with them."

"I don't know," replied her mother, "what Mr. Benson would say to that speech, Helen, for he thinks every one who has a fraction of money ought to be able to make the best use of it."

"That is what I dislike him for, mamma; not as a man, of course, but as a lawyer. I suppose they are all alike though—a dry, clever, questioning, puzzling set, who seem to make what they persist in calling the simplest things so difficult to understand; and they frighten one into believing that things are a great deal worse than they really are, just to make themselves appear more clever, I suppose."

" I shall certainly have to repeat this long speech of yours, Helen," said her mother, "and leave Mr. Benson to reply for himself and friends. I have no doubt he will be glad of an opportunity to teaze and mystify you, to make up for the long rest he has had: he does, I know, enjoy a little quiet fun at your expense.

" Now, mamma, love, don't, I beseech you," replied Helen, earnestly. " You know how he frightens me; and I shall never learn to like him better if he continues to catch at every little thing I say, and make it appear foolish. Every one cannot possibly be as clever as he is, or as you are, mamma; and laughing at my failings will never help me to overcome them, I am sure."

" Why, my dear Helen, I was only joking; you surely know that; and, after all, it is only manner with Mr. Benson: he is most kindly disposed towards you: of course he would be for your father's sake, if for nothing else," replied her mother.

"I dare say you are right, mamma; but you will allow he has rather a singular way of showing it. I will try to overcome my dislike to talking with him, only do promise not to say one word to him about me."

"Well, Helen, I will not, as you wish it, though I confess the temptation is great, as you appear so alarmed; but be upon your best behaviour when you meet him at dinner to-day, which is half-an-hour earlier than usual; and I hope the Clennings will be punctual."

The subject of the above conversation was a shrewd, clever man, who had an excellent connexion and practice. He had applied himself with unflagging energy and patience for many years to all the nicer and finer points in his profession, and seldom failed to carry through with success the

many weighty and difficult matters put into
his hands by his trusting clients. He certainly had not a pleasant manner, especially
to young people; he was very satirical, and
turned into ridicule any harmless, innocent
expression they made before him—more to
annoy and vex them, because they allowed
him to see that he could do so, than
perhaps from any real ill nature. He was
also brusque and dictatorial, two of the
weaknesses of human nature which do not
add to any one's amiability; in fact, it was
generally allowed, that in spite of all his
extreme cleverness, he was decidedly bearish
to his fellow mortals. Perhaps very clever
men cannot help, as a rule, making others
feel how ignorant and stupid they are. The
fault may not be all theirs, however. It
may be that our very ignorance and
stupidity prevent us from understanding or
appreciating their more gifted conversation
and manners, and cause us to prefer the

society of our less clever friends. This was Helen's feeling towards Mr. Benson. She knew how kind a friend he had been to both her mother and father, and yet she would always have gladly avoided seeing him or saying a word to him.

During her father's illness, and when he was in difficulties about his loss of money, Mr. Benson had first come to see them. He had then undertaken, at Mr. Leigh's earnest request, to become a sort of guardian to his child; and perhaps it was this which had given him the idea that he had a right to give her, whenever he saw her, the full benefit of his sharp, sarcastic remarks, which had filled her girlish fancy with a wholesome dread of him; and as she grew older it scarcely diminished in the least. Mr. Benson had a great respect for her mother. No one had admired her husband's strict integrity and painstaking industry more than he

had; and he always spoke with evident
satisfaction of their close friendship. But
his visits never lasted over a day or two,
so Helen was soon relieved from his disagreeable presence. He left them the
following morning after an early breakfast.
"Good-bye, Helen; I trust you will take
advantage of Miss Clenning's offer of Gyp,
and mount her every day: a woman
that's afraid of a bit of blood isn't worth
a straw," was his parting speech.

"Helen, love," said Mrs. Leigh, a few
days after Mr. Benson's departure, "I have
been thinking that it is time we were
hearing something more from Kate. I
can't find her last letter, but I fancy she
said she would come to us about this time,
and I should like to know what day she is
certain to arrive."

"Oh, yes, mamma, so should I. She
might have written to me before this, 'tis
true, though no one ever knows much

about her movements beforehand; she always does everything differently to other people; and because she is so positive herself, and decides so quickly, she takes it for granted that every one knows as well as herself what she intends to do," said Helen.

"That may be all very well sometimes," replied her mother; "but it is not always convenient for any one to come unexpectedly to us."

"I should not wonder at her coming in any moment without saying another word about it, mamma."

"Oh, nonsense, Helen; she surely will telegraph when she crosses, at least; somebody must meet her. I do wish Kate would try to be more particular in these little every-day matters. I am afraid she is dreadfully spoiled," said Mrs. Leigh.

"Oh, mamma, dear, nothing of the kind. Kate could not be spoiled under any circumstances; she is too stately and

grand for such a thing to happen to her.
I quite envy her that happy, easy way
she has of managing others, without the
slightest apparent effort on her part,"
replied Helen.

"Kate is certainly not nervous, Helen,
I allow; but that very manner you seem
to admire so much ought, I think, to make
her more attentive to the ordinary duties
of life, and not so careless and difficult to
understand," said Mrs. Leigh.

"Oh, but, mamma, dear, it is only
because you do not know Kate as well as
I do that you do not understand her.
You will alter your opinion before she goes
away again, I feel certain," said Helen.

"Well, I hope so too, Helen, for I like
her very much in spite of her failings, and
am very glad she will come in for the
festivities at the Clennings," replied Mrs.
Leigh.

"So am I too, mamma. She will

delight Mrs. Clenning, I am sure, and win all their hearts at first sight. She is so fond of gaiety, that I fear, with all her admiration for you, mother mine, and her love for me, she would tire very soon of our quiet, steady-going life, and long to leave us to the uninterrupted enjoyment of it," said Helen, gaily, " unless we amuse her very well indeed."

All this bright anticipation of her friend's visit may have been enjoyable enough to Helen; but to her practical, methodical mother it was certainly rather perplexing not to know positively whether or not this delightful young creature intended to honour them with her presence. Having a great desire to make everything in readiness for her guests, and as Kate was not the only one she was expecting, it would have been pleasanter to have known when she was coming, and how long she intended to stay.

Helen resolved, if no letter came that day, to write in the evening; but, fortunately, the afternoon bag brought news for them. The young lady excused her apparent neglect by saying that her father had been so far from well that she had not liked to decide to leave home, but that he was now going on quite nicely, and, time and tide permitting, she hoped to have the great pleasure of being with them some day the following week,—most likely on the Tuesday.

As she is to be much talked of in this story, a few words will be necessary about her previous history and relations; so before she comes to her English friends, we will try to be better acquainted with her, and she shall form the subject of our next chapter.

CHAPTER II.

KATE BYRNE was the name of the friend Ellen Leigh and her mother were expecting to visit them. She was the only child of an Irish gentleman, and had been motherless from early infancy, as Mrs. Byrne had died soon after her birth. The sorrowing father centered all his great love and care upon the little one who had cost him so dear, watching her with almost more than womanly interest and tenderness during the anxious years of childhood. He had the satisfaction of seeing her grow up a strong, healthy, beautiful girl, devoted to him and her aunt, Miss Casteldi, who had come to live

with them after her sister's death, and who
had been as near like a mother to her niece
as it was possible for any one to be. Of
course Aunt Neta was the dearest aunt that
had ever lived, in Kate's opinion, and no one
had ever had such a good, kind, indulgent
father.

It will easily be believed that Kate was,
between them, sadly spoiled. The slightest
wish or whim of hers had always been readily
given way to under any circumstances, and
it certainly would not have been a matter of
great surprise if she had grown up thoroughly
discontented and unlovable. At eighteen,
when she returned from school, she was tall,
and a decided Irish beauty, with lovely, dark-
blue eyes, and an abundance of black hair,
which she wore in close coils around her well-
shaped head. Her complexion was clear and
fresh, her manners quiet and dignified, and
there was a certain nameless something about
her, which made people turn, and look again,

and wonder who and what she was. She had, perhaps, just a touch too much pride to be always pleasant to those around her, especially if they did not know her well.

Only at times did she show that she had inherited from her mother all the passionate warmth of her Southern nature. It was not little things which put her out of temper. She either laughed at them, or thought them not worth even that; but several times during her girlhood she had given way to bursts of temper and angry feelings which had made both her father and aunt extremely anxious about her future, and had caused them to send her away from home for two or three years to a school in England, from which she came back improved in every way, and delighted with her school life.

Everything had been easy and pleasant to her. None of the drudgery that so many girls complain of had been felt by her; in fact, she was one of those fortunate people

who seem to have no difficulty in learning
and doing easily all the various things, the
knowledge of which does so much, in most
instances, to refine and cultivate the mind
and manners, and make agreeable friends
and companions in society. Her loving
father was especially pleased with the improvement in her voice—which was full,
and rich, and clear; and as he was a very
good musician, he looked forward to having
great enjoyment with her. Some slight
kindness shown by her to Helen Leigh,
soon after the latter had gone to the same
school, had at first brought the two together
on a friendly footing, and this had ripened
into a strong girlish attachment, which
they both hoped would be kept up all their
lives.

Helen had visited Kate in Ireland during
some of the holidays, and the latter had
returned her visit, as Mrs. Leigh was
naturally anxious to see the young friend

whom her daughter thought so much of.

Mr. Byrne was particularly pleased with Helen. She had such gentle, winning manners, that he hoped she might have some influence over the impetuous daring nature of his beloved Kate, and he readily and gladly encouraged the interchange of visits between them. Mrs. Leigh was fully alive to all Kate's failings, but, in spite of them, she could not help being interested in the motherless girl, who was, with all her faults, very kind-hearted and generous. Kate thought Mrs. Leigh the nicest and best of mothers, and had often told Helen that she ought to be so proud of her, for, she added, "She is just what I would choose my own to be if I could have one."

Mr. Byrne's house is brilliantly lighted up one evening, about the same time as this story commences, and a peep into the inside would tell one that company is expected. Presently carriages begin to arrive, one after the other, in rapid succession, setting down the fair and fashionable occupants, who were received by the hospitable host, his sister, and daughter.

Kate does, indeed, look lovely, and her father may well feel proud of her as she stands by his side, radiant and happy, dressed in a soft-coloured rich silk, with a good deal of cloudy lace and tulle about her neck and arms. Black velvet bands were on her throat and wrists, and a tiny circlet of plain gold in her dark hair. It was her first grown-up birthday party, as well as a kind of good-bye before she left for her long visit to England. Since her return from school they had had several musical evenings, and Kate's voice was much admired and a good deal talked about. The rooms on this evening filled very quickly; the buzz of many voices became louder and louder, till it was almost impossible to make oneself heard; then Kate made a move to the room beyond, and sang again and again, at the oft-repeated requests of her visitors.

Among those who came late was a young Mr. Blake—Bartle Blake he was generally called by every one. The warm welcome he received from Mr. Byrne showed he was a favourite with him at least, which, in fact, he was, and also a constant visitor at the house. He had not been there quite as often of late, as he had been a good deal occupied with arrangements about an appointment he had received in Russia. Some friends had interested themselves very much indeed for him, as they knew he was clever and pains-taking,—just the steady kind of man wanted for the position; and one who would, in all probability, with such a start in life, do very well indeed, both for himself and his employers. Congratulations met him on every side, and no end of good wishes for

his future success; and certainly, for a young
engineer to have secured such an opening
for himself was something worth receiving
compliments for.

"How is Miss Byrne? I do not see her
anywhere. I hope she is quite well?"
Bartle asked of her father.

"Oh, yes, thank you. Kate never ails
anything, Bartle. She was singing just
before you came in, and must be there
somewhere. She will be very glad to see
you, I know, as she has been quite anxious
to know if you were the successful one,"
replied Mr. Byrne.

No man could possibly have been thrown
so much as Bartle had been with Kate
Byrne without feeling very much more
than admiration for her; and as he was no
"greater paragon of marble virtues" than
most of his brethren, the consequence was
that he became desperately in love with her.
He had gone on blindly allowing himself

to indulge in every opportunity he had of being with and near her, sometimes hoping that she knew all he felt, and was not averse to it; and then his bright hopes would be suddenly dashed to the ground by her cold, haughty manner, if he presumed to be the least tender or lover-like.

He was quite as proud as he was poor, and knew he had nothing to offer her but his unalterable love; but he was young and strong, and a few years could not possibly make any difference to her in her youth and beauty; and how much more easily he could work if he only could have the assurance of her bidding him hope, he thought.

At one time he would determine most positively to himself not to run the risk of breaking the charm of their intimacy by look or word, hard as it was to be near her and not do so. Then again he would resolve, come what might, he would tell her that she was all the world to him. But through all these conflicting thoughts one other was always before him, and however much he tried to fancy it was absurd, or shake it away from his memory, it remained in spite of him; and that one thought was, that Kate Byrne would never marry him,—no, not even if he was dying for love of her. Of course everybody said they were engaged. What other conclusion could people come to after seeing them for nearly two years so constantly together? But the old proverb could have been quoted in this case, and more truly applied with a little "*not*" before the last word. If all the events in this life turned out as our friends sometimes arrange for us in their own special way, how full of gratitude we should need to be for all the labour and thought they give to us and our affairs, without even the slightest intimation on our part that we need them.

As Mr. Blake makes his way to the end room, exchanging greetings with the people he knows, he sees Kate's tall figure in the conservatory beyond, and he finds her in close animated conversation with a certain Captain, of whom he has always been intensely jealous. He makes his excuses for being late, retaining the loved hand as long as he dare, saying that he had been kept waiting some hours for an interview with a man he was obliged to see; that he had hastened the moment he got away; and came there at once.

"I am so glad to see you, Mr. Blake; it seems quite an age since you were here last. My father misses you very much, and so does auntie. I won't say that I do, for fear of making you conceited," she added, smiling, as she placed her hand on his arm, and left the Captain to find another companion.

"Do you know that I am going away to-morrow for two or three months?" Kate said, as they walked round the flowers.

"Aunt Neta, and Norah and I, cross by the afternoon boat."

"Oh, surely not to-morrow?" replied Bartle. "I am sorry. I thought you were not going till the end of the month. Can't you wait a little longer, and then I can, perhaps, be of use to your aunt and you?"

"Indeed, I am quite able to take care of myself, and auntie too, for that matter; and I have already put Helen off some time on papa's account, so I could not possibly alter the present arrangement to please any one but myself," replied Kate.

"Oh, but I can't bear the idea of your going alone. I will try and hurry my affairs, if you could wait without real inconvenience; I would then see you all safely across. I have so much to say, that—"

"Pray do not trouble yourself, Mr. Blake," said Kate, interrupting him quickly; "we do not require any one's assistance; so do not hurry, at least on our account, I beg of you; there is not the slightest possible necessity for your doing so, I assure you. But there is papa. I must go to him," she added, as she passed before him, and made her way to the piano again.

Bartle followed, and stood close behind her, sad at heart, for there was something in the tone she had said those last few words that brought back all his doubts and fears. If she really cared two straws about him, would she, could she, treat him in such a cold, off-hand manner, especially knowing that there would be so few chances of their seeing each other again for some years? One short stay at a friend's house near where she was going to visit, and then he would have to say farewell for no one knew how long; and yet she positively refused to allow him the pleasure of crossing in the same boat with her. He tried to under-stand all this as he listened to her sweet voice, and noticed the admiring glances of

the other guests who were near; and so
deep was his wondering, that he almost
started back when Kate, having finished
her song, and bowed her beautiful head to
the many thanks and remarks of her hearers,
turned round to him, and said,—

"Now, Mr. Blake, please, before it is too
late, do you sing something. One of the
old songs, for a change. Shall I play for
you, or will you accompany yourself?"

Bartle thanked her, and seated himself at
the piano. He had a good deal of musical
talent, and had also had, alas! for his future
peace of mind, too many opportunities of
practising and improving his naturally fine
voice. He sang that beautiful air from the
'Trovatore,' "Non ti scordar di me!" Never
did Mario charm the ear of maiden fair
more, when singing that air, than did Bartle
Blake, on that last evening in her own home
with him, Kate Byrne's. The guests were
all gone, she was in her own room alone,

having dismissed the faithful Norah, she
stood leaning her elbow on the mantel-peice,
with her head resting on the fair, jewelled
hand. How full of thought she seemed,
how different the expression on her young
fresh face, that had so lately been all smiles
and animation! Perhaps if Bartle could
have seen her thus, and known what her
thoughts were, he would have made sure
of his future happiness.

"Non ti scordar di me" kept ringing
in her ears, and she exclaimed, as she
moved away from the place where she
had stood so long,—"No, never! Come
what may, in all my life I shall never
forget this evening, that song, or the
singer."

Somehow sleep did not come as quickly
as usual to Kate. She lay awake and thought
of Bartle for a long time.

"How I wish he was rich and great!
I could love him then; I do even as it is

D

a little. I think he is so nice, so good to papa, and I am certain he loves me very dearly, though he has never said so in plain words, and I hope he never will, for I am sure I should refuse him; for how *could* I marry a man who has neither position nor money, and, perhaps, never will have till he is quite old and not able to enjoy it. I almost wish I was not going to see him in England; it will be very hard to say no, I dare say, but I must have wealth and position if ever I do marry: life with a poor man would be unendurable after a few days or weeks, perhaps, so I will never endanger my peace of mind by making such a mistake."

Thus thought Kate. She did not, however, dream of putting the question to herself as to whether she had all this time been giving encouragement to him; seriously she never thought of her own actions, and she fell asleep wondering how it would end, and believing that whatever happened it would be no fault of hers. How easy it is for us all to cast away from us any belief in what we do not wish to own even to ourselves. It is not *always* difficult for us to answer the "still small voice" which will whisper to us at times, and force us to frame some excuse for our shortcomings.

CHAPTER III.

THE next day was fine and clear, with not very much wind, the sea just rough enough to let one know that one was on it; and among the passengers by the fine steamer "Connaught" were Miss Casteldi, Kate, and Norah. The preparations for departure were being hurried on, and Mr. Byrne and Bartle were waiting to take leave of the three travellers. Kate was as full of spirits as ever; there was not a shadow of a sign of last night's cogitations to be seen on her bright face. She was enjoying a little quiet bantering, telling them she hated a smooth passage, when they pity her for the tossing she will get the next four hours.

"If I could have my way," she said, "I would always have it very rough. I don't, of course, wish to go to the bottom, papa, love, but I do like to feel that the sea is grand and powerful,—quite beyond the puny efforts of man to stay or curb its fury. I love to watch it, too. If I had been born a boy, I should have run away if you had not let me have gone to sea, papa, I feel certain."

"My darling, I dare say I should not have said no to even that," replied her father; "but where is your aunt?"

"Oh, gone, and snugly ensconced by this time in her berth, I have no doubt, papa, and going through agonies in anticipation," replied Kate.

"I will just step down to her for a moment, if you will stay here, Bartle, till I come up," said Mr. Byrne.

"I do so wish I was going, too; I feel almost tempted to run over to-day and return to-morrow," said Bartle.

" Oh, nonsense," replied Kate; " don't
waste the last few precious moments in useless suggestions, but go, if you please, and
see where Norah is, that is, if you really
wish to oblige me."

Of course he wished to do the slightest
thing she asked of him, and went to see after
Norah, wishing, at the same time, that that
worthy young person and all her belongings were at some far-away place it would
be scarcely polite to mention. He soon
returned, followed by Norah, bearing tri-
umphantly a small box which an energetic
porter had tried to claim as the property of
another passenger.

The good-byes were at last obliged to be
said. Mr. Byrne took an affectionate leave
of his daughter, who, as she shook hands
with Bartle, hoped to have the pleasure of
soon seeing him again in S—shire, and then
the handsome vessel steamed proudly out of
harbour with her precious freight, who were

waving their adieus to their friends on shore.

Kate went down to see that her aunt was comfortably settled, and if she could do anything for her. But, no; Miss Casteldi only wished to be left alone and quiet, and tried to induce Kate to stay downstairs.

"My dear aunt, I should be ill immediately if I did," Kate replied; "it is the very worst thing one can do, I assure you. To stay on deck, however rough it may be, is by far the wisest thing; the fresh breeze is invaluable for keeping one right. Don't mind me, I have a book, and shall take no harm, while you and poor Norah submit to your less fortunate circumstances."

She arranged her aunt's pillow and went on deck, where she tried to read, but found the wind and spray too strong for such enjoyment; so she wrapped her cloak closely round her, drew down her gauze veil, and walked about, busy fancy giving her quite enough to occupy her time. She wondered if Bartle would go back with her father, and make himself as much at home as he usually did when she was there; if they would talk of her, and miss her very much. Her father would, she knew; he always called her his sunbeam, and never was half so happy when she was away; and she felt almost as certain that her father's young friend would feel her absence even more than her father did. She was deeply grateful to him for his kind attentions to them all. How much her father would miss him when he went to Russia! So would she when she returned home again. It would be so strange not to have him coming and going constantly, with his bright, cheerful manner and ready help; no one could do so well all the little attentions that they had been accustomed for so long to receive from him. What a pity he was so poor! What nonsense to say that "Money is the root of all evil," when there is scarcely a good thing that can be done without it in this world! Love in a cottage was all very well in theory, and did for school girls and boys. To her life would be simply unendurable if she could not have all the luxuries and amusements she had always been accustomed to. Life was too short to waste on the desert air, and surely there could be no harm in wishing for those indulgencies, the possession of which she was born to enjoy and appreciate so thoroughly. Then her thoughts roamed away into the far future, which she could but hope would be as bright as the past had been, and as the present is, for her. "What is to be, is," was one of Kate's pet mottoes; and as she could never give herself very long to reflection, she quoted it to herself, and turned her thoughts to more every-day matters, as she watched the fine, full waves of the beautiful sea they were gliding over.

Perhaps the reader may think that, for a girl of nineteen, Kate is very worldly and selfish; that her ideas are extremely unmaidenly and wanting in refinement. This may appear so, but is not really the case. She is not, certainly, what some would call a model woman; on the contrary, she is full of faults and failings, which are doubtless more the result of the spoiling manner in which she was brought up than of any natural wickedness of disposition; and it must be allowed that it is not an uncommon circumstance for women to prefer both power and money to the much-talked-of and rarely-to-be-found true love. When such is the case, it is scarcely fair to blame them for accepting what to them would be their greatest happiness, and infinitely more preferable than all the adoration which could be lavished upon them. If love could be combined with the former, then, of course, it might add greatly to the enjoyment of all parties concerned; but if not, let them choose whatever they think will conduce most to their future peace of mind, and do not let us blame or judge them from any set standard of our own that we may chance to think the correct one.

"Mamma," said Helen Leigh, "I've a short note from Kate, who is leaving Chester this morning, and hopes to be with us this afternoon. Her train gets in at four, or a few minutes after, she says. Can we go and meet her?"

"Oh, certainly, Helen. We will both go; and James can take the dog-cart for her luggage, if you think that will hold it all," replied Mrs. Leigh.

"No, mamma, love, I do not. Kate always takes quantities of things about with her. We can see about it, and send for it afterwards," said Helen.

"What a lovely day for her! I will order

dinner a little earlier. She will be glad of it, I dare say, as soon as she comes; it is a long journey. I will see at once about it and the carriage. Does she say how her father is?"

"No, mamma, not a word. But he is, of course, quite well again, or Kate would not have left home. Miss Casteldi is going to Broughton for the present, and will join us in a week or two—that is all," answered Helen.

"But not to take Kate away for some weeks I hope, Helen? I know her aunt is so restless away from home."

"I hope not, indeed, mamma. We must have our own way this time," replied Helen; "and I quite forgot to mention to you that Julia Clenning told me yesterday her papa met Mr. Blake in London, and made him promise to come and pay a short visit to them before he goes away altogether."

"I am indeed glad to hear it, Helen. He was a mere child when I saw him last. He came to visit us in Manchester with his mother just before you were born, Helen." Mrs. Leigh did not notice the bright blush that spread over her daughter's face, but went on telling stories of this boy's sayings and doings on this particular occasion, which Helen listened to and laughed about with as much good nature as if she had not heard them again and again.

How is it that most elderly people (especially gentlemen) seem to have such pleasure in the constant repetition of their pet jokes and stories? How wonderfully good-natured their listeners need to be to show any sort or kind of interest, or listen with patience to what is so very old and often very stupid! How is it that it never by any chance seems to occur to them that they have told the same thing often before to the very same people, with just as much earnestness and relish as at the first recital? However, it is one of the privileges of old age to be forgetful and garrulous, so we may hope that those who are young now and polite listeners will, when old age comes, find, in their turn, those who will do unto them as they have done unto others.

Helen busied herself with arranging flowers in Kate's room, having managed rather cleverly to coax more than usual out of their old gardener, who, every time there was a demand for some from the conservatory, gave them with an injured air, and in niggardly quantities, generally saying " it was a shame to cut 'em."

She then went to the Vicarage, to talk over school matters with Mr. and Mrs. Clayton, with whom she had become a great favourite; and thence she went on to Clenning Hall, where Mr. and

Mrs. Clenning, and their three daughters and only son, lived, and with whom Helen and her mother were on very intimate terms. It was only an easy walk from Mrs. Leigh's house,—The Ridgway, as it was called,—and the young people frequently walked over in fine weather to see each other. On this occasion, Helen had been asked to come to give her advice and any suggestions she might have about the arrangements for some festivities that were to go on in consequence of the coming of age of the only son and heir, which was to be celebrated in the most hospitable fashion, and no expense or trouble was to be spared. There was a large park and grounds, and every facility for the tenantry and guests to enjoy themselves. The difficulty was not *how* things were to be done, but *what* should be decided on as sufficiently worthy of so auspicious an occasion.

Mr. Clenning was an easy, good-natured man, very much attached to his wife and children, a good landlord, and a pleasant neighbour and friend. He gave way in almost everything to his wife, just because he did not care to be worried about things he could not understand. He disliked being made a prisoner of by her, and asked innumerable questions, and what he would do in such and such a case, because he said,—"My dear, you never act upon the advice I give you; you always do as you please whatever I say, so why waste my time and breath for nothing?" He was a keen sportsman, and very fond of his horses and stables, where he spent a good deal of his time. The consequence of this was, that Mrs. Clenning and her daughters were often left to their own devices; and Helen found them all in the library with their steward settling the weighty subject under consideration.

Mrs. Clenning was one of those martyrs we all sometimes meet with, who fancy — or, perhaps, it is better to say believe —that she had more to do, and really did more, than any other creature in this wide world could do under similar circumstances. This was, alas! a sad mistake of hers. To perplex and mystify those about her by the vagueness of her plans and her in- decision was what she did continually. What she resolved to do or have done one moment she would alter the next, then groan and get angry because nothing seemed to get done. In such an estab- lishment as hers, with her numerous de- pendents ready to do her bidding, every- thing ought to have gone on smoothly and quickly. But, no! from the top attic to the pantry she altered this and re-arranged that over and over again, and yet got no real satisfaction or rest after all her efforts, but looked upon herself as a solitary instance of a weak, burdened woman, with the affairs of all belonging to her to manage, and no husband to help her in the least. She did not think that the remedy lay in her own hands. If she would only have allowed people to help her, there were plenty ready and willing to do so.

As to her husband, no wonder, poor man! that he had refused of late years to subject himself to such silly nothings. He had borne it, no doubt, as long as he was able, and showed his good sense by giving up any attempt to coerce or guide her. Not being able to worry Mr. Clenning, of course her, daughters and Mr. Smith had come in for a very fair share of it on this occasion; but this morning everything must be decidedly settled, as it was late enough to put the preparations in hand.

"Ah, my dear Helen," exclaimed Mrs. Clenning, as the former entered, "I am

so delighted to see you. Sit down near
me, love; I want to talk to you. Such
terrible worry for my poor head, which
you know is not strong."

Helen sat down and expressed her sorrow
for the poor, weak head.

"Well, Helen, love, you are always
kind; tell me what you think of this plan.
The tenants' ball as well as the dinner on
Will's birthday; then our own dance the
following night; then the volunteers'
dinner and games in the park; and we
thought of a concert and picnic at the end
of the week, with a bonfire and illumi-
nations, as well as on the first day, of
course. Now, do you, my dear Helen,
think that will be enough? Tell me truly,
dear?"

"Oh yes, quite enough, and very well
arranged," replied Helen. "So much better
than crowding in so many things, which
there would be scarcely time for. Mamma

was saying she hoped you would not try too
many different amusements."

"That is an immense relief, my dear,"
replied Mrs. Clenning; "and I think we
will let you off now, Mr. Smith," she added,
turning to her steward, who quickly made
his bow to the young ladies, and withdrew,
no doubt fearing a re-call if he did not get
out of the way immediately.

"My dear Helen, I value your dear
mamma's opinion so much, I assure you,
that, if she agrees with me, I always think
I have done quite the right thing. I do,
indeed, my dear."

Mrs. Clenning was always overpowering
with her "dears" and "loves." Most
women of her character *are*, perhaps, more
or less so; and, although she did value
Mrs. Leigh's opinion very highly, there is
no doubt she had, at the same time, a still
higher appreciation of her own.

"What a mercy it is, to be sure, that one

has not a son coming of age every day!"
Mrs. Clenning went on to say. "I am
quite wearied with anxiety about everything. I dare say the weather will be
wretchedly dull and wet though as soon as
we are ready, so that the out-door amusements will have to be put aside altogether;
and, of course, the fireworks won't go off
if they are at all damp, you know, Helen,
love."

"Oh, mamma, please don't anticipate such
disasters. You will quite alarm Helen,"
said the eldest girl, Julia; "the weather is
lovely just now, and will remain at 'set
fair,' I feel persuaded, if only to oblige us,
and everything will go on quite properly
if you don't worry yourself about them."

"Ah, it is all very well for you, Julia, to
talk and think in that careless fashion, and
to be so positive and happy; but some one
must do the planning and altering; and as
your papa refuses to have a voice in these

matters, why the onus of the responsibility
falls on me, as a matter of course."

"But, mamma," said Annie, her youngest
and favourite daughter, "everything is
settled now,—no alterations *can* take place,
—so you will have some days of perfect rest,
I hope, before any of our guests arrive."

"I shall certainly try to take all the rest
I can, Annie, love, and prepare myself for all
the bustle and confusion that is to come.
And Helen, dear, about your friend, Miss
Byrne; when do you expect her?" said Mrs.
Clenning.

"This very day," replied Helen. "We
are going to fetch her about four. I so long
to see her again. It is just a year since I
was over there."

"Ah, how time flies, to be sure. But I
must leave you girls now, and go and lie
down; my head is splitting at this very
moment. Good-bye, Helen, dear; remember
me to your good mamma and Miss Byrne,

and bring her here as often as you can. I
shall be so glad to see her at any time."

"Do you think, Helen, that Kate Byrne
will help us in our *tableaux vivants*—we
were just saying that we should want a tall
dark beauty for some of them?" asked Julia.

"Yes, I am sure that anything of the
kind will just delight Kate. She used to be
first and foremost in those things at school,
and did them so well," answered Helen.

"How delightful!" replied Mary. "We
will all ride over to-morrow morning, Helen,
and offer her Gyp for her use while she is
with you."

"Do," replied Helen ; "but I must away.
Mrs. Clayton has offered to drive me home.
So good-bye for the present. Don't be late
to-morrow, and we will stay in till you
come."

"Mamma, isn't it kind of the Clennings,
they are going to lend Gyp to Kate ? Julia
says she will be so glad to have her use her,

and take some of her spirits out of her," said Helen to her mother, at luncheon. "I am so glad, as Fairy is by far too sober for Kate's taste."

"They are all very good-natured, indeed, Helen, and especially attentive and kind to their poor mother," replied Mrs. Leigh.

"Well, mamma, I cannot see why Mrs. Clenning requires so much forbearance and patience. She does really make such trouble of the merest every-day trifles, and orders those girls about as if they were little brain-less children, that I almost lose my temper with her; and how they bear it always I cannot imagine."

"You must remember, Helen, she is very delicate, although she always keeps about, and surely her children ought to bear with her peculiarities," replied Mrs. Leigh.

"Of course, mamma, you are quite right, I know; but then there is no real need of all this commotion about everything,—it only wears herself out, and other people too. She spends all her strength, and most of her time, in useless repinings," replied Helen.

"I dare say, Helen, Mrs. Clenning has trials that we know nothing of. She is not sanguine, I must admit; but we have all our weaknesses in some shape or form, and we cannot at all times prevent ourselves from letting others see them."

"I hope I have not been hard upon Mrs. Clenning, mamma. She is always so kind to me, that I should be sorry to say severe things of her. I was just thinking of what I heard there this morning, and pitying her girls, and felt thankful for having such an unselfish, thoughtful darling as you are for my mother," said Helen, kissing her.

"I will drive over to-morrow morning, Helen, while the girls are here, and see Mrs. Clenning, it is much longer than usual since my last visit there; and then I can thank her for Julia's kind offer to Kate."

CHAPTER IV.

RS. LEIGH and Helen were on the platform, waiting the arrival of the "iron horse" which was to bring their expected guest. The huge machinery had scarcely come to a stand-still before Kate was in Helen's arms.

"Oh, you nice thing!" she exclaimed. "How delighted I am to see you again, dear Mrs. Leigh. How well you look; and Helen, too, fresh and fair as ever, I declare."

"Why, Kate, you can scarcely have expected to find me very much older in a year," replied Helen.

"Oh, no, of course not, my blue-eyed Helen," said her friend; "but every one is

telling me how altered I am, though I confess I cannot see it myself."

"Nor I either," replied Mrs. Leigh, "except, perhaps, you are taller, and a shade
thinner, I fancy."

"Please don't tell me that, if you love
me, Mrs. Leigh; I have such a dread of
being thin and scraggy. I always fancy
people who are so are dreadfully disagreeable and crotchetty," said Kate, laughing.

During the drive to The Ridgway, she
kept up the conversation merrily with glow-
ing accounts of all she had done since she
last saw Helen. She was very much interested to hear of all the gaiety that she
was coming in for during her stay, and
offered to do anything in her power to
help the Misses Clenning.

"You have heard, I dare say, Mrs. Leigh,
of Bartle Blake's good fortune," said Kate,
in the evening, as she left the piano. "We
were all so pleased about it, though of course

his going away will be a great loss to our circle."

"Yes, I dare say he will be very much missed by every one," replied Mrs. Leigh; "still it is a fortunate thing for a young man like him to get such an appointment. When is he coming to Mr. and Mrs. Clenning? Do you know?"

"Not exactly," replied Kate. "Some day next week, I think; but I shall know when papa writes to me, I dare say. He is sure to mention it, I think."

"Oh, it does not matter, Kate, thank you; I only asked as it seemed uncertain whether he would come or not, and some one suggested that perhaps he would cross with you and your aunt," said Mrs. Leigh.

"He did offer to do so, if we waited a day or two; but of course we did not care to do that, as we are so well able to take care of ourselves, and pride ourselves upon being thoroughly independent," replied Kate.

While this conversation was going on at The Ridgway, the subject of it was sitting over the wine at Mr. Byrne's table. He had been asked by the latter to take pity on his lonely board, and to come and dine with him. It was quite natural that after dinner, when the younger man had fully discussed his own future plans, the conversation should turn to the absent ones.

"Is there anything I can take over for Miss Casteldi or your daughter?" asked Bartle, fidgeting with his wine-glass. "I shall be glad of any commissions."

"Well, no thank you, Bartle," replied his host, "I think not; as far as I know, they have left nothing behind them. Kate is careless, but her aunt is very methodical, and has a good head for remembering everything."

"But you can't quite expect Miss Byrne, sir, to be as thoughtful at her age as her aunt is," said Bartle.

"Certainly not, certainly not. My darling girl is all a father's heart could wish. I miss her sadly, I assure you, Bartle, and am always anxious about her when she is away from home, although I would not be so selfish as to wish to keep her from seeing her friends and enjoying herself."

"I can quite understand the feeling you have," replied Bartle. "Any home with your daughter to grace it must, indeed, be enviable."

"Ah, she is a good girl,—a little hasty, perhaps, sometimes. I think we have rather spoiled her, and my only grief is that I may be soon taken from her, poor girl! She is young to be left alone in the world. If I may say so," said Mr. Byrne.

"But, my dear sir, this is a very gloomy view to take of yourself; you are not feeling ill again, I trust," said Bartle.

"Oh, no, not at all, thank you," replied Mr. Byrne. "But you don't know, Bartle, what is wrong with me. I have been very careful not to mention it even to Miss Casteldi, as I dread the effect upon Kate if she were to hear of it. I am not right here, Bartle," he added, placing his hand on his heart.

"Oh, but my dear Mr. Byrne," replied his young friend, " people live to a good old age with that complaint, especially if they take care, so I trust you may be spared to us many years yet."

" Of course, I hope the same for my child's sake, if for nothing else," replied Mr. Byrne. " Elliotson has warned me for some time to be very careful, as any excitement may be fatal to me: this is why I go about so little with my daughter, and why I am always anxious about her when she is from home."

" You are just a little low-spirited to-night at their being away," replied Bartle, cheeringly ; " and no wonder that you miss them ; Miss Byrne's absence would be felt anywhere, I am certain. I feel it myself, and long for the time to see her again."

As his friend made no reply to his last remark, Bartle went on to say,—" To gain your daughter's affection has been my one great wish for a long time, sir, and, if you do not object to me, I shall tell her how dear she is to me before I go away."

" Why, my dear Bartle," said Mr. Byrne, rising from his seat and laying his hand on the young man's shoulder, " I had not an idea of this; you have taken me quite by surprise. Surely I might have known—so often together—quite like brother and sister for so long. My dear boy, I have looked upon you as a son, but I never thought of this."

Mr. Byrne seated himself again, and was silent for some moments; he then said,—

" Does Kate know of this?"

" I have not yet spoken to Miss Byrne, although I have felt certain that she is aware of my attachment," replied Bartle. "If you will give her to me, sir, my one great aim shall be to make her life as happy as she deserves."

"I believe you truly, Bartle," said Mr. Byrne. "I do not know any one to whom I could entrust my child's future with more confidence; but in this one great event of life Kate must be entirely free to choose. I cannot, even by a wish, attempt to influence her. She is one of those independent creatures who are best left to their own decision; but if you have any reason to believe that she returns your affection, why ask her, man; you have my most earnest wishes to attend you."

This conversation gave rise to a good deal of wondering and thinking in Mr. Byrne's mind. Had Bartle any real right to fancy Kate loved him? How strange it was that he had been so blind! His imagination was full of things which had happened in the

last two years, and to which he had paid
little or no attention; they were now so many
proofs of Bartle's growing affection for Kate
to her anxious father. For some months
past, in spite of his efforts to shake it off, a
gloomy kind of presentiment had hung over
him ; first and foremost about his own health,
and then concerning Kate's future. He feared
that, if he were called away, she would have
so much more to contend with, and no one to
understand and appreciate her. He could not,
even to himself, account for all this ; he only
knew it was always present with him night
and day. Sometimes the oppression was so
great that it almost alarmed him. Then,
again, he would manage to reason himself
into a more hopeful state of mind, and think
that these fears were, perhaps, only the
natural consequences of his ill health. Then
he would begin to hope he had been wrong,
and foolish in allowing himself to brood over
the imaginary ills of the unknown future;

but he never entirely lost his anxious feelings even for a short time. Who can say
that we do not all sometimes have shadowy
glimpses of coming trouble? If such a thing
has never happened to us, we all surely know
of instances where these forebodings have
been most singularly and painfully realized.

Mr. Byrne felt that if Kate cared for Mr.
Blake he should be very much more satisfied
about her. He knew him to be so thoroughly
honourable and kind, that her happiness
would be quite safe in his keeping. And,
of course, if she did love him, nothing need
interfere with their plans, as they were both
young enough to wait a few years, if there
was any necessity for it. The idea that his
lovely child might, perhaps, allow ambi-
tious, sordid views to influence her for one
moment in the choice of a husband, never
entered his head. She was too proud, too
refined, to barter the holier and purer feelings of her nature for wealth or position.

This would have been Mr. Byrne's reply if any one had ever suggested to him that she might possibly do so. What he "hoped" she was, he easily made himself believe a real positive fact; and nothing could have pained him more than the knowledge of there existing a single individual in their whole circle of friends who would not have agreed with him in everything he thought about her good qualities.

When Mr. Blake arrived at Clenning Hall the following week, he saw Helen and Kate, just saying "Good-bye" in the porch to the Misses Clenning, so that there was only time for a hurried "How do you do?" as Mrs. Leigh was expecting them back to dinner, and they were already very late.

"You will come and see mamma, Mr. Blake, wont you?" said Helen. "Her recollection of you goes back to a very remote period, I assure you; she will be so glad to see you again."

" Oh, certainly; it will be a great pleasure for me. May I come after dinner if I can get away ?" said Bartle, as he assisted them into the pretty pony-carriage which was waiting at the door, and arranged the slight dust-rug around Kate, who, whip in hand, was ready to dash off in her usual stylish manner; but as she wanted to ask a question or two about her father and friends, she allowed him to walk by her side down the drive, where they again said, " Good-bye" for the present, and she was borne rapidly out of sight by the impatient ponies.

" What a queenly creature Miss Byrne is," said young Clenning, as they turned to go to the house; " and how splendidly she rides and drives, doesn't she ?"

" Yes, indeed, there is no doubt she does," replied Bartle, scarcely knowing what he said, and looking absently at the boyish figure by his side. He made many apologies to his host and hostess for leaving them his first evening, the temptation of seeing Kate again was too strong to permit him to lose any chance that came in his way; so he and young Clenning walked over quickly in the fine May evening. Mrs. Leigh received him very warmly, saying, as she held his hand and looked at his tall figure,—"Dear me! Is it possible that you are the tiny boy who came to my house more than twenty years ago with your mother?"

"I believe I am the very same, dear Mrs. Leigh," Bartle replied, laughing, and seating himself as near to Kate as he possibly could; "only I have been obliged to obey the laws of nature, and increase considerably in stature since then, I allow."

"Oh! Mr. Blake," said Helen, smiling archly, "mamma tells several stories of your youthful delinquencies which are very amusing. You really alarmed her one day, when your own mother was out, and—"

"Oh, hush, hush, Helen, love!" interrupted

her mother; " it is not fair of you to repeat those things. But do not notice what she says, Mr. Blake, I beg of you."

" I certainly feel ashamed, dear Mrs. Leigh, that at any time of my life I was ever such an ill-behaved little mortal. I have not, however, the remotest recollection of the circumstance; but if my ill deeds have grown with my growth and strengthened with my strength, I must by this time be a near approach to a monster of iniquity," said Bartle, good-humouredly; and, turning round to Kate, he asked her if she did not agree with him. She scarcely looked up from the delicate lace-work which she held in her fingers, and replied,—" Well, I really do not know what to say about it, Mr. Blake. I might be severe, and agree with you, as I make a point never to flatter any of my gentlemen acquaintance."

" But," replied Bartle, pointedly, " truth seldom flatters, I think, Miss Byrne; and

surely no one has a right to be offended if
they hear it, especially from a friend."

" There, I do not agree with you," replied
Kate, quickly. " It is often very unpleasant
and annoying, I 'm sure, and simply unendurable from a ' friend,' as you say. One
could bear it ever so much better from a
stranger, I think."

" I see you have misunderstood my meaning entirely, Miss Byrne," replied Bartle;
" but we won't say anything more about it
if it annoys you."

Kate turned an indignant quick glance at
him as she moved to fetch something from a
small table near her, as much as to say,—
" Annoy me, indeed! you are quite mistaken."

Helen and Mrs. Leigh wondered what had
vexed their young friend, as she had been
in such high spirits before the young men
had come in; but they took no notice whatever, and went on asking and answering

questions, till Helen proposed some music, and the evening passed quickly and pleasantly, although every one felt that Kate was not in very good humour. Before they went away, Will Clenning arranged to come over early the next morning, and take the ladies to see the games in the park; and, as a matter of course, Bartle offered to come with him. As soon as their visitors left, Kate pleaded headache, and went immediately to her room, assuring Mrs. Leigh, in reply to her anxious inquiry as to whether she was ill, that it was scarcely worth mentioning, and a good night's rest would make her quite free from it. But Kate dismissed Norah in a sharp tone; and, instead of retiring to take the needed rest, she read and thought for a long time, and then resolved to punish Bartle Blake for his impertinence before he went away. The truth was, that he had been so taken up with Mrs. Leigh and

Helen when he first came in (which, considering the time that had elapsed since he had seen the former, was hardly to be wondered at), and having seen Kate at the Hall only an hour or two before, he had scarcely noticed her, beyond bowing to her as he entered. Now this apparent neglect had piqued and annoyed her more than one would imagine, and the above unamiable resolution was the consequence.

The next day was fine and warm, and the amusements were quite a success. They were all entered into with great goodwill by both guests and tenants, and Mrs. Clenning had the grim satisfaction of knowing that, in spite of all her predictions to the contrary, everything went well, even the unfortunate fireworks, which had so distressed her since their arrival. Dancing was kept up till a late hour that night in the large tent, which was beautifully lighted with Chinese lamps, whose number was legion. William Clenning had always been a great favourite at home ; and though he was not quite as brilliant as he might have been intellectually, he was, perhaps, the more amiable for that. At all events, the cheering and good feeling that his pre- sence seemed to call forth on that especial birthday were very hearty and genuine. His appearance in the dance was the signal for a tremendous " Hurrah ! " and " God bless him " ; and it made the pretty village girl with whom he danced more than once feel, perhaps, a little too important, if one might judge from her rosy cheeks, bright eyes, and coquettish manners.

The young folks mustered numerously about noon the next day at The Ridgway —the three young ladies from the Hall, with their brother and guest, Bartle Blake, Helen, Kate, and another visitor. Every one was in good spirits, and had some· thing funny to say about yesterday's doings.

Kate and Helen had both been writing, and, as the latter got up to put her letter-case away, a tiny silver-edged envelope fell from it.

"Oh!" exclaimed Helen; "see, girls, these are Janet Parker's wedding-cards. You have seen her here once, I think; she was one of our schoolfellows,—a pretty, fair girl, and as good really as she was or is pretty."

"Yes," replied Kate, passing the cards to Mary Clenning, "so 'good' that she has married a poor curate, who I suppose has nothing but his extreme 'goodness' to recommend him. Curates are always wretchedly poor, and she has no fortune of her own to speak of, I know; so I see nothing for them both but real hard work, which she, at least, is not fit for. I have no patience with girls being so imprudent."

"Why, Miss Byrne, you might be, I

declare, fifty years old, and speaking from bitter experience," said Annie Clenning, laughing. "When two people love each other, they don't think of these small matters, I suppose."

"Small matters, indeed! At all events, these very small matters are what ought to be considered and acted upon, for I am sure, if *I* married a poor man, I should hate him in a few months," said Kate, decidedly.

"Oh, no, you would not, I feel certain, Miss Byrne," said Julia; "that is, if you loved him with all your heart; and of course no one in their senses would marry if they did not, I should think."

"Heart!" exclaimed Kate; "as if that had anything to do with the matter. For my part, I don't believe in such things. One loses all that school-girl nonsense as one gets older, I trust, and looks upon that part of the human frame in the same

light as the Scripture does, which, if I
remember rightly, says, 'The heart is de-
ceitful above all things, and desperately
wicked.' Isn't that it, Helen?"

"My dear Kate, you are not serious, I
can see. I cannot believe that you have
such views in reality; and—"   .

"A great mistake, Nellie," interrupted
Kate. "I do truly believe what I have
just said; and moreover, I maintain that
the less we talk about the possession of
such a doubtful belonging the better; so
pray don't look so very incredulous and
unhappy, or I may say a great deal more
to surprise you."

"Well, Kate," replied Helen, "I could
sooner have believed any one else I know
would say such things than you. I always
fancied you above mean ideas."

"Did you really, you sweet thing? Call
them mean, if you please,—I can bear it
from you; but I must add, that your

thinking thus of me is only a proof that what I say is true, for without trying to deceive you, I evidently have, as far as the state of my morals is concerned," said Kate.

"Well, Kate, I shall still hope you only fancy all this, and shall be able some day to prove to you that it is just chit-chat, nothing more. I know you of old," replied Helen.

"As you please, Nellie; I promise to humbly own myself in the wrong. But suppose we say no more before Mr. Blake and Mr. Clenning. The former will not be at all edified with our nonsense, I am sure; and will Janet, who gave rise to it, require my pity, if she is to be so dreadfully happy?" asked Kate.

"I do not suppose for one moment she will either require or thank you for it, Kate," said Helen, severely.

A servant coming in, put an end to the talking, and they all separated soon after, arranging to ride in the afternoon, and then meet again in the evening, when the large ball was to take place.

As the party returned to the Hall, Mr. Blake and Mary Clenning were companions. He appeared to listen to her scraps of news and her remarks about their friends, but he really paid little attention to anything she said, for he was turning over in his mind every word that Kate had said in the library. If she *really* felt as she tried to make them believe she did, he had indeed little to hope for.

CHAPTER V.

MONG the numerous guests who were staying at the Hall was a certain Lord Denton, a large landed proprietor and distant neighbour of the Clennings. He looked about forty or forty-five years old, was stout, not very tall, and altogether in appearance more jolly than gentlemanly. He was not often to be seen at Denton Court. During the shooting season he would come, perhaps, with a few gentlemen friends, and stay for a few weeks; then he would be off again for months, or till the same season came round again.

The Court was a large, roomy place,

and had been comfortably and handsomely
furnished; but since the present master
had come into possession, one-half of it,
at least, had scarcely seen daylight. Very
little was really known of Lord Denton's
past life. Of course, busy Rumour had no
end of tales to tell of him and his doings,
not one of which was more reliable than
the other. He had been desperately in
love, when a young man, so the story ran,
with a young, beautiful girl, very much
below him in station. He had told his
father that he intended to marry her if
she would have him; and his father had
insisted upon his breaking off all inter-
course with her, threatening, if he dared to
go a step further, or see her again, that he
would disinherit him. Soon afterwards the
girl married some one else,—and it was
added that she had received a handsome
sum of money to do so from the father
of her lover, who had persuaded her to

go to America, and that she had never been seen or heard of since.

Another story was to the effect that Lord Denton had been jilted by a young London beauty in a most heartless manner, after the settlements had been made, and that, in consequence of this last cruel blow, he had sworn never to believe or trust in mortal woman again henceforth and for ever.

He was so often away that no one seemed to know much about him,—what he did, or where he went. The management of his estate was entirely left to an intelligent bailiff, who, to do him justice, looked after the tenants and their wants a good deal better, perhaps, than his Lordship would have done if he had lived more at home. He was not very popular, as may be supposed; but, upon the whole, he was generally allowed to be generous and open to reason by his tenantry, and a jolly

kind of fellow, only too fond of roving,
by his friends.

Managing mothers had wasted a good
deal of precious time in trying to catch
opportunities for their daughters to storm
the stronghold, and thaw his Lordship out of the icy regions of celibacy,
but all to no purpose. Denton Court
remained half shut up and without a mistress. The aforesaid mothers ceased to look
upon the event as ever likely to take
place, and wisely spared themselves any
further unnecessary trouble or anxiety
about him, and consoled themselves by
repeating to any fresh acquaintance any
trifling bit of news, old or new, which
did not reflect great credit upon his Lordship's past life.

He was a capital rider, and always kept
a few horses at Denton. It was a kind
of nursery for the invalids; and it was
his coming to bring and see after a recent

valuable purchase that had enabled the Clennings to invite and persuade him to accept their offer of a few days' visit during the coming-of-age festivities.

Of course the Clenning young ladies were very pleased to have such an un-expected addition to their guests. No one had even dreamed of his being there, so rarely was he to be seen among them; and they all agreed that " something " would happen in consequence.

Mrs. Clenning declared most emphatically that she was certain he would only send a message to say he was called away upon business, or something of the kind, as every one knew he made a point of never going anywhere when he was asked. But she found herself on this occasion very much deceived, and, we must hope, pleasantly surprised, by the appearance of this most un-come-at-able person. For the short time he stayed with the ladies after dinner the

first evening he made himself so agreeable,
and was so much at his ease, that no one
would have supposed he went little into
society. He appeared to know everybody
and everything, told many amusing short
anecdotes of his foreign travels and experi-
ences, which, to quiet country girls such
as the Misses Clenning, were very interest-
ing, and they all voted him charming.
Mary told a young friend confidentially
"that now the ice was broken she dared
venture to say they would see a good deal
more of him than they had ever done
before; and as there is only a sickly life,"
she added, "between him and a dukedom,
I believe, if he would only marry and
come into it, it would be very much better
and nicer for us and the rest of his
neighbours."

"He plays billiards splendidly," said
young Clenning. "It was quite a treat to
see him handle a cue, and we all stayed

till the small hours became rather large."
This remark, by the way, was offered as
an excuse for putting in a late appearance
at the breakfast-table the following morning.

When the dancing commenced in the
evening, Mrs. Clenning hoped she would
have the pleasure of introducing Lord
Denton to some agreeable partners, and
every moment was watching the door
thinking each fresh-comer was Mrs. Leigh
and her young people, who she had
hoped would come early. However, he
assured that painstaking lady that she need
not trouble about him at all, as he never
danced now-a-days. If Miss Clenning would
excuse his blundering, and allow him the
pleasure of the quadrille just forming, he
would be very pleased; and then he would
so much rather stay quietly and watch
the rest."

"Mark my words, Annie," said Mary,
"if Lord Denton does not rush off presently

to those abominable billiards; he keeps too near the door to be quite safe."

They were, however, mistaken in their surmises about him. He really had no wish to run away; on the contrary, he was very much taken up with watching Kate Byrne's elegant figure gliding round the room with their young host. She had on a soft, rich amber silk, with black velvet and gauze trimmings, and looked exceedingly handsome and animated as she passed him, chatting gaily with her partner between the turns in the waltz.

"Who is that tall, dark girl in amber-coloured silk, Mrs. Clenning? She was dancing with your son just now. There she is, sitting beside one of your daughters," said Lord Denton.

"Oh, that is Miss Byrne,—a friend of a near neighbour, Mrs. Leigh; you know her, I think. Miss Byrne is quite a beauty, as you see, and very popular everywhere, I assure you. She comes from Ireland, and we have all taken a great fancy to her here," said Mrs. Clenning, in reply.

"Perhaps you will introduce me to her whenever there is an opportunity. She is very distinguished-looking, certainly. Byrne, Byrne,—I seem to know the name quite well," replied his Lordship.

"Her family is a very good and a very old one, I know, and her mother was a beautiful Italian of noble birth," said Mrs. Clenning, as she moved away to where Kate was sitting, followed by Lord Denton. "Miss Byrne, let me introduce you, love, to a neighbour of ours, Lord Denton."

Kate bowed her head slightly, and, in reply to his request for a dance, gave him her dance list; but he found few vacant spaces, and those very far down. He made himself as agreeable as he possibly could to her and her friends, and managed to get on much better with Mrs. Leigh than

with Kate; but her quiet, indifferent replies,
instead of making him fancy her proud and
haughty, as so many others did when they
first met her, enhanced her whole appearance
so much, that before very long he thought
her the most beautiful creature he had ever
seen, and far superior to any woman he
knew or had known all his life. Her glorious blue eyes quite fascinated him, and he
found himself longing for his turn to become
her partner.

Kate had been hearing something of his
history from one of the Misses Clenning,
and had resolved to show the utmost indif-
ference to any attention he might pay her
when Mrs. Clenning brought him to her.
But she found that he really had a way of
ingratiating himself in her favour, and she
really talked to him a good deal at the end
of the evening. There was but one opinion
among the company, and that was that at
last Lord Denton was fairly smitten with

the charms of the bright, blue-eyed Irish girl.

What Bartle Blake's feelings were on the subject may be more easily imagined than described; he, of course, with Love's jealous eyes, saw all that went on, and after the conversation in the library at The Ridgway, he could but look upon Lord Denton as a dangerous rival. He was rich, and able to offer all the luxuries this world can give; and there was no doubt about the impression Kate had made upon him. Of course Bartle could not enter into the enjoyments of the evening very thoroughly; but, though his mind was in a state of great disquiet, he affected to appear at ease, and made himself so agreeable and attentive to his fair partners, that no one could have guessed his secret annoyance.

After the company had all departed, the three daughters of the house went to their rooms for a few hours' rest; but, as usual in such cases, they were obliged to talk over the pleasures of the evening before they retired to bed.

"What a success this dance has been," said Julia, as she put some finishing touches to her hair before the glass. "Every one has seemed to enjoy it so much, and we had plenty of good dancing-partners, which was a comfort for us all, and not half as much trouble for mamma and me; and if Lord Denton is not desperately smitten with Kate Byrne, my name is not Julia Clenning."

"I hope so," replied Annie, "and that we shall have a wedding soon, and all of us be invited to it, with lovely lockets to console us for being left still in the blissful state of spinsterhood. He is just the most delightful man I know, and shows his good taste in admiring Miss Byrne. I don't believe a word they say about his hating women, and all that nonsense—do you?"

" I can't say," replied Julia; " people of course always exaggerate those kind of reports. There may be very little truth in any of them; but I think it is rather singular that he should make his first visit to us just when she is staying in the neighbourhood."

" Well, having met him here, if anything does come of it, the least she can do is to ask us to be bridesmaids. I shall never forgive her if she does not," replied Annie.

" How absurdly you go on, Annie. We may be quite mistaken; but, whether or no, she is a most charming acquaintance, though I confess I think she is rather vain," said Julia.

" I can quite forgive her that, seeing how much excuse she has for being so. I always look upon vanity as the least objectionable weakness that flesh is heir to, and were I Kate Byrne I should be simply unbearable with conceit," replied Annie.

As Annie finished her sentence, Mary, the younger sister, who had not taken part in their conversation, said, in a very sleepy tone of voice,—"You are both mistaken, girls, clever as you think yourselves. I don't wish to deny that Denton may have fallen a victim, but, take my word for it, Kate Byrne loves Bartle Blake, and if they are not engaged, they soon will be. You may get your locket, Annie, but not from a future Lady Denton. So good night, or good morning, I should rather say, as it will soon be daylight. No beauty sleep have we had for the last week, I declare. Have some thought of to-morrow, and don't sit up any longer,"—and, giving them each a kiss, she left them, with her new idea to think over.

The next day was the one for their picnic at St. Albans. A large riding and driving party started from the Hall, calling on their way for Mrs. and Miss Leigh and Miss

Byrne, the former having seats in the waggonette, and the latter riding Gyp. Helen always avoided riding whenever she could, as she was very nervous and easily frightened, especially with Kate, "for she generally makes her horse tricky," said Helen, "and then I immediately fancy mine is going to be so too, and suffer dreadfully, only to be laughed at afterwards by her."

Mr. Blake helped Kate to mount, and rode by her side for some distance; but that pleasure had to be resigned to another, and he fell back to the other young people, and joined in their gaiety, although he was really very miserable. Kate had been so totally different to him the last few days, that he again and again regretted having come at all. He could have gone away with at least pleasant recollections of their life in Ireland, which would have been far better; for Kate had done nothing but snub him, and he had scarcely done or said a single

thing to please her; and now that Denton
was taking up all her attention, it was almost
impossible to get one word from her. The
day was sunny and warm; all nature was
bright and happy; the birds and flowers
were enjoying and adding to its beauty,—
and yet he, one of God's noblest creatures,
was so miserably discontented, that he was
wishing heartily he were dead. However,
Fortune favoured him soon after luncheon,
for Will Clenning declared that none of
the good walkers must return till they had
climbed to the top of a hill in the distance,
from which a splendid view of the sea and
the surrounding country could be had, which
it would be a thousand pities to miss, as the
day was so clear. Lord Denton declined
climbing the hill, so he stayed behind to
take care of the ladies who were not going,
he said. Either by chance or design on the
part of the young ladies, Clenning, Miss
Byrne, and Bartle were left some way

behind. The road was rather rough and
fatiguing; Kate stumbled against a stone,
and exclaimed as if her foot was hurt, stand-
ing quite still for a moment; but in reply
to Bartle's anxious, tender inquiry, she said
it was nothing, and went on, refusing his
offered arm.

"Thank you, I have quite as much as I
can manage with my habit; I didn't think
of that when I offered to come, or I would
have stayed behind with the rest."

"I am very glad you did not, though,"
replied Bartle. "I have seen so little of you
lately. You don't know how I have longed
for the chance of a quiet chat with you.
Lord Denton has come in for a very full
share of your company."

"Has he really?" replied Kate, with
her face as white as a sheet. "Indeed,
I was not aware of it; but he is certainly
extremely agreeable and nice,—quite different to what one has heard he is; but

then one should not listen to idle tittle-
tattle."

" I agree with you entirely. Still I know
there is a good deal of mystery about his
doings for the last few years, and he is
scarcely a man I should have fancied you
would take to," replied Bartle.

" How can you possibly have an idea of
whom I should ' take to,' as you call it? As
to Lord Denton, he happens to be rather
more agreeable than most men, and that is
all I really care a straw about; therefore,
you need not try to say ill-natured things of
him, especially as he cannot hear you, and
defend himself. After all, I dare say he is
no worse than his neighbours," said Kate,
carelessly.

" I have no doubt," replied Bartle, " that
he would be delighted to know he has so
lovely a champion, but I don't want to waste
words or time on him. After all that has
passed between us, you must know how

much I love you, Kate, and how I have longed for months to tell you so. Just one word, darling, will make me the happiest man in creation—if it is only ' Yes.' "

Kate changed colour, and did not reply at once. Her heart beat so fast, that had her life depended upon her uttering only one single sentence, she could scarcely have done it at that moment.

Bartle gained confidence by her silence, and went on passionately, hurriedly telling the " old, old story " over again.

" After all that has passed between us, you say, Mr. Blake," she said, making a great effort to speak calmly. " *I* know of nothing that has passed between us,—except that, from the welcome my father always gave you to his house, and the kindness he has shown you, I had an idea I might freely give you my friendship, never supposing for one moment that you would misconstrue it, as you evidently have done, and put an end, as it must now do, to the sisterly feeling I have always had for you."

" Then I have, indeed, made a terrible mistake,—as far, at least, as I am concerned," replied Bartle. " Stay one moment, Kate," he added, laying his hand on her arm, as she hastened on at a much quicker pace, and turned an angry glance upon him. " Your father knows of this, and has told me I have his full consent. I spoke to him the evening of the day you left home, when I dined with him."

He hoped that the mention of her father's name, whom he knew she loved very dearly, would soften her; but instead of having that effect, it made her more angry, and she replied, haughtily,—

" Did you indeed, sir ? Thank you. In future I would advise you to be rather more sure of the lady's consent before you ask her father's."

This appeared so thoroughly rude and

heartless to Bartle, that he immediately resolved not to attempt to say another word. He merely bowed to his angry companion, and walked the rest of the way in perfect silence.

They found all the others seated on the top of the hill, enjoying the scenery and resting. Will Clenning sprang up as soon as he saw them, and, throwing his cap high in the air, shouted, " ' Excelsior!' Here you are at last, you two,—such laggards. Isn't it a pull up here, though? What a lovely sea to-day. Wouldn't it have been a pity to miss this? I'm quite tired; arn't you?"

These and such like expressions greeted Bartle and Kate. The former made laconic replies, but Kate was out of temper, and took no pains to hide it. She fancied that they had purposely hurried on and left them, and saw, she thought, telegraphic signs and looks between them all as soon as they made their appearance.

She would not sit down to rest, but advised their all returning as soon as possible, as it looked as if it was going to cloud over and rain. The truth was, she longed for the solitude of her own room, where, away from every one, she could think in peace and quiet.

"Oh, Miss Byrne," said Julia, "it isn't going to rain, I feel certain; with such a sky it is simply impossible; but, as you say, we ought to be getting down again, as it is later than I thought. Time goes so quickly when one is pleasantly engaged, doesn't it?" she asked of Kate, who made no reply.

"How dreadfully pale you are, Miss Byrne! Whatever is the matter? You are limping, too. Miss Leigh, do come here." Helen turned back, and saw at once that something had happened to her friend.

"Kate, love, what is it?" she asked.

"Oh, nothing to make a fuss of Nellie.

If I am so pale I really cannot help it.
I have hurt my foot, and I don't know
how to lift it from the ground, that is the
real fact. But there's no help for it. I
must get to the foot of the hill, where I
will wait for the carriage, if you will send
it on for me."

"Can't we carry you, Miss Byrne?—
Blake and I?" said a young man of the
party. "If you would let us, we could,
I'm sure."

"Oh, no, pray don't say a word to the
rest. See! they are looking round at us
now. Do go on, and I will manage somehow."

The "somehow" was painfully difficult,
and when she had reached the bottom she
was really quite exhausted and faint. Mr.
Blake, and Helen, and one of the Clenning
girls, waited there with her till the waggonette came with Mrs. Leigh and Mrs. Clenning, who brought some wine with them.

"It was stupid of me, I dare say, to go on walking after I twisted my foot, but I hoped the pain would go off. It was not so bad at first, and I hate to make a fuss. I shall be all right when we get home."

There was some difficulty in getting into the carriage, and the drive home was long and tedious to Kate. The whole party were not quite in such high spirits as they had been when they came along the road in the morning.

CHAPTER VI.

"AKE care, Norah, I beseech you.
I cannot bear that. You had
better cut off my boot, I think;
don't you, Mrs. Leigh?"

Mrs. Leigh saw directly that
Kate's foot was terribly swollen, so she
immediately sent for Dr. Andrews, and
gave orders for a room to be got ready at
once for Miss Byrne downstairs. Kate, in
the mean time, lay on the sofa in the
breakfast-room, quite pale, and suffering
great pain.

"I can manage very well, dear Mrs.
Leigh, with Norah's help, to get upstairs,
if I go at once, I think. I would really
rather try to do so, and then I shall be

more out of the way, if I am to be a prisoner for a few days, which, I suppose, will be the case," said Kate.

"May I for once, my dear Kate, decide what is best for you to do? You will be better down here for many reasons; and I can do the same for you as I should for Helen under the same circumstances with much less fatigue," replied Mrs. Leigh, decidedly.

Kate felt inclined to rebel, and wished herself in her own dear home, where one word from her was always sufficient for instant attention to her wishes and orders; but somehow it was impossible for her to dispute with Mrs. Leigh, or to resist her tender, motherly affection, so she allowed herself to be treated, as she said, "like a baby," and submitted to being installed in the room in question.

Dr. Andrews arrived in an hour or so, and pronounced the sprain a very bad one;

indeed, he said that it would require a
good deal of time and patience to enable
Kate to use her foot again, or even to put
it to the ground.

"Oh, nonsense, Dr. Andrews; I shall be
able, surely, in a few days to get about
again? I dislike so much to be all day long
in the same room."

"Well, my dear young lady, you may be
carried for change of air and variety into
the drawing-room, if you like; but I must,
indeed, positively forbid any attempt at
walking or moving for at least a week or
two," replied the doctor; "that is, if you
wish to give your foot a fair chance of
recovering."

"Well, then, dear Mrs. Leigh, since
Dr. Andrews is so cruel and so determined
to punish me, you must send me home as
soon as he will permit me to move ever
so little, for I shall become quite unendurable, and tax even your patience

beyond bearing, with so long an imprison-
ment."

" We shall see, Kate ; time works
wonders," replied Mrs. Leigh. " Of course,
if you behave very ill, we shall be obliged
to spare you ; but I would rather keep' you
till you are quite strong again."

As Helen went past Kate's room that
night, she fancied she heard her call out
to her; but having said good night before,
she thought she must be mistaken, and
went on upstairs. But Norah followed
her, and said that her mistress wanted to
see her; so Helen returned, and Kate said,
—" Oh, Nellie, dear, do sit down and talk
to me a little, please. I feel certain I
shall not get to sleep at all, my foot pains
me so much. I could cry out with sheer
agony, if it was not for the shame of doing
so. This has been such an unpleasant
day. I wish I had not come near the
place at all."

"Oh! Kitty, love, don't say so," replied Helen, seating herself, and taking her friend's hot hand; "don't say so, pray. You have been the one bright star amidst us all; and to-day, too, we all thought you had thoroughly enjoyed yourself, in spite of this misfortune. Before you hurt yourself, and independent of it, the day was not unpleasant, was it, dear?"

"Yes, it was," replied Kate, snappishly. "I hate picnics; they are always a bore to me under any circumstances; and I shall never forget this wretched one all my life long, I am certain."

"Oh, yes you will, Kitty, when you are better. You are hot and feverish now, and your head aches, I am sure, very much indeed. Do try to go to sleep; that will do you so much good. I will go now and send Norah to you directly, so good night again, love."

"Don't go yet, Nellie. Why are you in

such a hurry? It is quite early yet, and I have so much to say to you. I want to tell you what happened to vex me to-day," said Kate, lowering her voice, and keeping hold of Helen's hand tightly, while she poured into her listener's ear all that had passed between Mr. Blake and herself.

" But, Kate, darling, is it a question of poverty or love? Do you or do you not love him? That is the proper light to look at it in, I should say," said Helen, slowly and earnestly, the fitful crimson coming and going on her cheek and brow. " What has his poverty to do with it?—he is quite worthy, I am sure, even of such love as yours."

" Oh, if you are going to be moral and lecture me, Nellie, I beg to be excused any more," replied Kate, leaving hold of her friend's hand and turning her head away; " at least just now I can't do with it. I am sorry I troubled you. I always thought it a bad plan for girls to tell these things to any one, however intimate they may be; *now*, I am convinced it is a great mistake."

Helen saw that Kate was in no mood to be reasoned with, and that it was useless to prolong the conversation even by trying to soothe her ruffled feelings, so she kissed her, and left her to Norah's care for the night. When Mrs. Leigh paid her an early visit the next morning, she found her looking almost better than she could have expected, as she had had little, if any, sleep; but upon the whole, she said, "she had not had a very bad night, and that if she kept her foot perfectly still, the pain was not too great to be borne."

Helen came to sit with her after breakfast, and, kissing her, said,—" How is the head, Kitty, now?"

" Quite well, thank you, Helen. I wish I could say the same of the heart, as people call it—I should say temper though, as a better way of expressing myself, if you will allow me. I am still a wee bit cross and spiteful, and how to get into a better frame of mind I know not. I am, however, sorry for being hasty to you last night."

" Don't mention it, Kitty. I haven't thought twice of it, I assure you. You have only to make the same admission to the much more unfortunate recipient of your anger yesterday, and your peace of mind will be restored at once, I vouch."

" I don't agree with you, Nellie," replied Kate, holding her forehead in her fair, white hand, and speaking thoughtfully. " I may confess my shortcomings to you willingly, because I love you very dearly, and am sorry to vex or annoy you; but there are very few, indeed, besides you to whom I could make the slightest advance after any misunderstanding, and I certainly never should dream of—. But there, I am saying more than I intended. We will never mention last night's subject of conversation again, if you please, Nellie; I want to forget it ever happened;

and I can only do so by not dwelling upon it. It is always better not to think of the unpleasant things that happen to one," she. added, seeing by Helen's face that she was expecting more confidential disclosures and discussions.

The fact was, Kate felt really more ill at ease than she had thought she should. As she lay awake in the night she had gone over and over again the scene of the previous day, and, in spite of all her reasoning and assuring herself that she had done no wrong, a "still, small voice" would whisper, "You know you love him; tell him so before it is too late."

It is just possible that if Bartle had called at The Ridgway that day, as Kate felt sure he would, the whole of their future lives would have been happier,—at least Kate's might have been; but he did not come near them. Every ring at the hall-bell, every footstep, made her listen for the well-known

voice, only to be disappointed, and wonder
why he did not, and when he would come.

"Mamma," said Helen, "do you know
that Mr. Blake has left the Clennings, asking
them to say good-by and make excuses to
you for his not coming? Some pressing message came from London late last night, and
he went too early this morning for making
any calls, although he must have passed
here, of course. I met Julia and Willie out
riding as I came from the school, and they
gave me the message for you."

"I am sorry not to have said farewell,"
replied her mother; "but I dare say he will
write to explain what took him away so
suddenly."

"Has Kate told you, mamma, what happened at St. Albans?" asked Helen.

"No, child. What do you mean, Helen,
love?"

Helen then told her mother what Kate
had said about her refusing Bartle; but she

begged her not to mention it to Kate if she
made no allusion to it herself.

" I thought, mamma, it would explain
Bartle's apparent neglect: of course he did
not wish to come here again. He is no doubt
very much pained at Kate's refusing him,
and I dare say a good deal surprised, for they
have seen so much of each other, and were
such good friends."

" It is most unfortunate if he really is
attached to her. I am rather afraid that
Kate is exacting and selfish, which is no
wonder, considering how every one spoils
her—ourselves among the number. I do not
see any cause for her refusing him unless her
affections are engaged with some one else;
he is quite a gentleman, of very good family
on both parents' sides. He is poor, certainly;
but I think he is almost sure to make his way
in the world."

" Oh, but mamma, I 'm sure, Kate will
never marry unless she gets the offer of a

title and wealth besides. She is so brilliant and fond of society, that she could
not live without every indulgence, I am
afraid."

" Then I am, indeed, sorry for her, Nellie.
I know of no worse fate than marriages of
that kind, unless, indeed, she combines love
with position, which, perhaps, with her beauty
and talents she may do. There are few men
who could see her and not be very much
charmed with her. I should think one does
not often see a girl so singularly gifted and
beautiful to look at."

Helen, of course, agreed with her mother's
last remark; but she felt surprised to see how
little impression Mr. Blake's sudden departure
made upon her. As to her own feelings in
the matter, she would have given a good
deal to have seen him, under any circumstances, only once again. But even this had
been denied her. She could not so much as
tell her mother how truly sorry she was

for him, and how she longed to be able to comfort him in his disappointment. No, she felt almost ashamed of being unmaidenly enough to have allowed her fancy to over-step the bounds of girlish dignity, and make her feel more than a common interest in one who never, by word or look, showed that he regarded her otherwise than as a friend. There was nothing left for her to do but lock the secret safely in her own heart, and try to appear as if she had it not.

The neighbours and friends who lived at all near to The Ridgway, called often to inquire after Kate; and she very gladly welcomed those who were inclined to stay and chat with her. One morning the three sisters from the Hall walked over, and offered to stay some time, and Kate asked them if they would like to hear a singular dream she had had the night before.

" Oh, by all means tell us, dear Miss Byrne," said Annie. " Julia is so clever

at interpretations: she has great faith in
dreams, too, and obliges us very often, I
assure you, with a 'meaning.' "

"Annie, you are too absurd," replied
Julia. " Don't notice her giddy nonsense,
Miss Byrne, if you please."

" Well, then, young ladies," said Kate,
" to begin at the beginning, as the story-
books say: I was, in my dream, seated at
the foot of a green sloping hill. Everything around me was beautiful, bright, and
gay; birds sang, flowers of every hue were
blooming in profusion and splendour; foun-
tains threw out ten thousands of jets of
sparkling water; lovely hills and dells, as
far as I could see, rose before me. No
other living being but myself was there. I
seemed to have no wish to move, but half-
sat, half-reclined, enchanted, as it were, at
the scene before me. Then presently I
heard soft, distant, trilling music. It
gradually came nearer and nearer, till I

thought I should soon see the players. But no, whichever way I turned to look there was no sign of any one. Then all at once I saw two bands of women and girls coming towards me; the music went on in exquisite melody: those who came first and quickest had in their hands lovely caskets and gems, which they laid at my feet as they passed me, saying, ' Come with us and be happy'; they were all beautiful, and their drapery· hung round them in thick, soft folds. The others came on slowly, and had nothing in their hands but flowers; but there was so much difference in their appearance, that I distinctly remember feeling they were all better and purer women than the others. They all held out their hands to me, and gave me their flowers as they went by, and I was so much more taken up with the brighter and richer offerings, that I scarcely heeded them, except as they gave them to me.

"I made no effort to rise till they were

all a long distance off, then I followed after
the first, who stood beckoning me from afar.
I went on, on, on, till I came to a beautiful
place, with men and women and children
all enjoying themselves in different ways;
but somehow I felt as if they were not
real; I had a kind of shrinking from them,
and yet I joined them in their amusements.
Men bowed low before me, and studied my
every look; then all at once I was enveloped
in a thick mist or cloudy darkness, which
frightened me, and made me cry out for
help. No one answered, but I heard mock-
ing laughter and derisive cries quite near.
I threw out my arms and moved slowly on,
till I felt grass on rising ground. I caught
hold of it, and tried to go up the hill, but
I could not see through the dimness, and
as I clutched one piece the other gave way,
and I seemed to go back after every step
I took. I had a kind of feeling that if I
got up that hill I should be safe; so I toiled

on, praying for just one gleam of light; but
no sound, no light came to me. The utter
sense of loneliness I felt I cannot possibly
describe : the hot tears of despair rolled
down my cheeks and fell on my hands, and
I thought of the bright scene I had just
before been in. I managed to reach the top
of the hill at last, where I saw a light down
on the other side—a dim, shadowy, melancholy one; and as I strained my eyes to
see, there were gaunt, hideous figures making
signs and grimaces at me. I felt there was
full, bright day behind me; but though I tried
to turn and go to it, I could not. I felt I
must go to these dreadful creatures : I could
not resist the impulse which seemed to send
me down. I screamed with horror and
misery, and awoke both myself and Norah,
who declared I had frightened her dreadfully. I was in a perfect state of fear and
trembling, and could not realize for some
time that I was really and truly in bed,

and that my distress was only a dream. I
found by my watch I had only been asleep
a short half-hour, so that it all must have
come and gone rapidly, although it seemed
to be ages in the dream."

"Why, my dear Kitty," said Helen,
"how singular, to be sure; but then you
don't sleep soundly now, and I dare say
the pain from your foot causes you to have
troubled slumbers."

"Oh, my dear Miss Byrne, what a
remarkably unpleasant time you had of it
altogether, quite like a visit to a world not
as pleasant as our own," said Mary.

"Well, what do you say about it all,
Miss Clenning?" asked Kate. "Has your
usual lively imagination helped you in this
instance to predict 'good' or 'ill' for my
future? Not being a direct descendant
from Pharaoh, I don't pretend to possess
any powers in that hidden art myself," she
added, smiling.

Julia reddened, and laughed too; looked very severely at her sisters for having put the idea into Kate's head; but she positively refused to say anything more than that it was very singular and disagreeable. They soon after went away, and, naturally enough, they talked a good deal on their way home of Kate and her dream.

"How beautifully she described it. I can almost see it all myself, and hear the music too," said Mary. "She looked so lovely, lying there with closed eyes, as if she was going over it all again in her mind's eye, while repeating it to us."

"Well," replied Julia, "there's a stormy future in store for her, or I am greatly mistaken. I could not tell her so, of course, but we shall see."

"Oh, nonsense, Julia; there you go, with your doleful dumps, as usual; so like you. I am glad you had sense enough not to say anything of the kind to her though. I never, till Miss Byrne mentioned them, thought of the Egyptians; but really I shall begin to fancy that there is a possibility of our having sprung from that race, if you put on that dreadfully puzzled and somewhat fierce expression very often."

" Thank you, Annie; it is just possible that they would not deign to acknowledge the connexion, if you tried to prove it—as far, at least, as you are concerned, miss. So don't trouble your frivolous little head with what does not concern you," replied Julia, severely.

"Who is this coming? Not papa or Willie, surely? No, Lord Denton. Going, of course, to The Ridgway," said Mary.

They stopped to shake hands with his Lordship, who said he was sorry to have missed them, and that he was on his way to call to inquire after Miss Byrne.

"We have just left her," said Julia; "she is in excellent spirits, but of course frets at being unable to get about."

"I wonder," said Annie, as he rode away, "what makes him look so spry and fresh, and why he is staying at Denton? I know he told mamma he should be off directly again; it is nearly a fortnight ago, and he seems in no hurry even now."

"*I* can't understand how it is that Mr. Blake and Miss Byrne are not engaged," said Mary. "I know he is passionately attached to her, for Will told me so; and men never say these things of each other unless they are true."

"Oh, don't they indeed!" replied Julia. "Mary, child, you know nothing about what they do. Men are just as apt to get hold of scraps of news, either true or false, and make as much of them, as we do, whenever they can get a little innocent like yourself to listen and appear to believe them. As you grow older you will grow wiser, and see the truth of what I say."

Lord Denton was pleased to find himself

admitted into Kate's presence, for though
he had called each day, he had not seen
her. He sat down near her, and compli-
mented her upon her appearance. "I am
afraid no one would think anything was
wrong with you, Miss Byrne, if they
judged by your face."

"I am sure they would not," replied
Kate, smiling. "It does seem absurd to
lie here and feel so well too. But, I
assure you, I am not to be blamed. For
once in my life I have no will of my
own: I am simply obedient to those around
me. Am I not, Mrs. Leigh?"

"Yes, you really are wonderfully patient,
Kate—*for you*, I mean," said Mrs. Leigh,
shaking her head, and laughing.

"That is very sweet of you to say so,
because it must be true since you allow
it, dear Mrs. Leigh. As far as my own
feelings are concerned, I am sure I could
hobble about somehow; but Dr. Andrews

wont allow it, so I try hard to show him and Mrs. Leigh that I really have a small *quantum* of obedience in my nature. My only fear is that I am using the little I have so lavishly that it will be quite exhausted, and no one else will ever have the benefit of any from me again."

"However, out of every ill comes a good, they say," replied his Lordship. "Perhaps if this had not happened we should not have had the pleasure of keeping you here so long, Miss Byrne."

"Oh, yes," replied Mrs. Leigh; "Kate came for a long stay, and we are expecting Miss Casteldi to join her here for a few weeks at least; then, I suppose, we shall have to let both of them go away to Ireland again."

Lord Denton stayed about twenty minutes, during which time the conversation was shared with Mrs. Leigh and her daughter about every-day events. When he took

leave, he held Kate's hand firmly in his
own, assuring her that this short visit had
given him very great pleasure, and begged
to be allowed to come again the next day.
As she looked up to reply, their eyes met,
a bright blush spread instantly over Kate's
face, and that one look made Lord Denton
go on his way rejoicing.

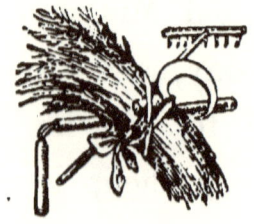

CHAPTER VII.

HEN Aunt Neta came to The Ridgway, she found Kate able to move about with comparative ease, and she had the pleasure of being driven about by her niece in Helen's little pony-carriage to see the beauties of the surrounding neighbourhood. The latter little lady was only too glad to have more time to devote to her beloved schools and "old people," as Kate called them.

"How you can possibly fritter away so much of your time and thoughts on such creatures I cannot imagine, Nellie," said Kate one day, when Helen came in quite tired out with teaching and visiting. "You look half dead at this present moment, and if I had any voice in the matter I would certainly put a stop to it at once."

"Oh, Kate, how can you accuse me of frittering away my time? If I do no good, it is not because I do not try to work hard; and you ought to be the last to say such things, when you know how much pleasure it gives me, and how anxious I am to do all I can for my less fortunate fellow-creatures," replied Helen, reprovingly.

"That is just what I mean, Nellie; you do a great deal too much—are too much taken up with those poor people; you do not consider what is due to your own position. Let those who ought to work exert themselves a little more. It is quite the proper thing for the wives and daughters of clergymen, I allow, but not for you," said Kate.

"But you know, Kate, I do what I can to help Mrs. Clayton. She is old, and not strong, and has no daughters of her own."

"Yes, I know you do; but why should you? You are not strong either; and you do not give yourself the leisure and pleasure that every girl ought to have,—that is what I complain of so much. I really wonder at your mamma allowing you to go so often into such dirty pokey places, where at any time you may catch fever and all sorts of horrid things," said Kate,—and her short upper lip curled disdainfully at the bare idea of the risks her friend ran daily.

"You are very much mistaken," replied Helen; "almost all the cottages are nice and clean; there is seldom or ever any serious sickness about,—such, of course, as to alarm one, I mean. If you only knew how much they appreciate any visits they get, you would think differently. It is because you never do anything of the kind that you

fancy it must be distasteful and useless for
any one else to attempt it."

"Oh, no, Nellie, I don't agree with you.
I am always ready to help any case of distress which is brought under my notice, as
far as my purse permits. And you may
depend upon this, dear, that nine times out
of ten money is more acceptable than any
number of visits; and I maintain that it is a
thousand times better to do what is easiest
to oneself without considering so deeply
what the results may be."

"It is just the way to do the most harm.
I know, Kate, if the poor do not like you to
see them in their own homes, there is something wrong somewhere; either they see
you are not at all interested in them and
their belongings, or that you only go to
find fault and point out defects."

"Well, well, Nellie, you won't be persuaded, I see," interrupted Kate; "and as I
cannot argue upon disagreeable subjects

without losing my temper, we won't say another word. I give in sweetly to oblige your little ladyship. Oh! there's the luncheon-bell; let us go and get something to eat, for you, at least, are looking much in need of a little wine to put a touch of colour into your cheeks."

"If I thought you really meant all you said, I would not be good friends till I proved to you how wrong you were," said Helen, as she took Kate's arm to leave the room.

"Oh, you unchristian young person. But I won't quarrel with you. Wait till you come to Blackrock again, and then we will see who is to be mistress. You shall lose your pale face there, at any rate."

Mr. Byrne began to get impatient for his daughter's return, and as she had quite regained the use of her foot, there was no real necessity for her staying away any longer. He had become tired and weary without

his sunbeam, he wrote, and was longing to
see her again; so Miss Casteldi decided to
go at the end of that week, or early the
following one.

Lord Denton also gave out again that he
was leaving the Court, and had requested an
interview with Miss Byrne before he did so.
There is no necessity to repeat what took
place during that interview. He had, from
the first moment he saw her, felt that she
was necessary to his existence, and knowing
that she was returning home, he feared to
risk his chance of being made happy with
a favourable reply by delaying till he saw
her again.

The readers will not be surprised to know
that Kate accepted Lord Denton's offer.
There was no show of affection on her side;
she allowed him to take the kiss he claimed
when she said " Yes," but drew herself away
from him when, in the excess of his happiness at being accepted, he would have taken

her to his heart, and assured her again and again how much he loved her. He had also something to tell her of his past life, which he had decided, before he made up his mind to propose to her, should and must be told then. But these things never turn out as we plan they should, and before he had time to begin, she had begged him to let her go and send her aunt to him. She was so very pale, that he feared she was ill, and tenderly asked her if he should call some one to come to her.

"Oh, dear no, thank you; there is not the slightest necessity for anything of the kind; the heat always takes my colour away: there must be thunder in the air, I think," she said, as she left the room. When she reached her own, she locked the door, and paced slowly backwards and forwards till she heard her lover's footstep on the gravel-walk; then she stopped, and thought again of another footstep that she

had waited, and listened, and longed for,—
of another scene, similar to the one that had
just taken place; and she felt that if "he"
had only come to her that day, and asked
her again to be friends and love him, she
certainly would not have been there at that
moment, and Lord Denton her accepted
lover.

Miss Casteldi was very much surprised
to learn from his Lordship that her niece·
had accepted him. She could not realize
the idea of such a thing, she said; and,
seeing his look of surprise, went on to
tell him, by way of excuse, that "Kate
is the sunshine of her father's heart and
home, and we never can look forward to
losing her with any feeling but regret. It
will be a great trial, especially to my
brother; though, of course, we must not
allow our selfish love to interfere with
Kate's future happiness."

"But I trust we shall always be able

to see you both very often," replied his
Lordship. " I promise you not to be a
tyrant and keep Kate away from her
friends," he added, smiling.

Of course, Mrs. Leigh and Helen con-
gratulated her, and wished her much happiness; and all their friends and acquaintances
appeared not to be the least surprised at
the turn affairs had taken. Each of the
Misses Clenning had her own opinion.
Julia was inclined to be severe upon even
the beautiful Miss Byrne, whom she really
admired very much, for captivating the
only eligible *parti* in their neighbourhood.
" Though, to be sure, perhaps if she had not
no one else would," she added, as she took
a side glance at her own rather handsome
face in a glass beside her. Annie was in
ecstasies. She was charmed at the thought
of having Kate Byrne for Lady Denton.
She knew there would be delightful parties
and balls at the Court, and a chance of

seeing a few fresh faces—both men and
women—she hoped. "And then, Julia,
who knows what may happen; besides, you
know, we are sure to go to the wedding,
and 'one' makes many, they say, don't
they?" she added, saucily. Mary was inclined to be hard upon Kate too; for
hadn't she made up her mind to hear that
what her brother had said was right, and
that she was to become Mrs. Blake at
some future time? If she had been Miss
Byrne, she would sooner have married Mr.
Blake without a penny piece than Lord
Denton with all his wealth. However, they
all allowed that it would be a great addition to the place having some life and
gaiety at the Court, which had been shut
up continually ever since they could remember; and they were all very anxious
to know as soon as possible when the
marriage would take place.

No one could suppose, from Kate's appear-

ance and manner, that she had decided
otherwise than happily. She was so gay
and so full of spirits, that it would have
been simply absurd to raise any doubts
whatever. She was anxious to get home,
naturally enough; and it was decided that
Lord Denton should cross with them on
the following Saturday. There could be
no doubt about Lord Denton's affection
either. He showed only too plainly that
he was the willing slave of Kate's capricious
fancy, and assured her again and again
that she was the first woman he had ever
loved. He would certainly have preferred
a little more demonstration on her part,
but he hoped, as she learned to know him
better, she would love him more, and then,
of course, she would show it, he hoped.

The night before they were to leave
The Ridgway Lord Denton had gone away
early, and they had all retired to rest before
the usual time. Kate had not returned to

her room upstairs, for it was thought best for her to go up and down as little as possible, so that she was still sleeping on the ground floor, with Norah in a tiny room beside her. For some reason or other, Kate could not get to sleep, although she was very tired indeed, and had made up her mind to have a good long night. After some time she did drop into a kind of doze, out of which she was awakened by hearing, she thought, something heavy fall either just outside or near her room. She sat up in bed and listened, but everything was so still that she began to fancy she was mistaken, and lay down again, more wide awake than ever. Then she caught the sound of subdued voices and a low grating noise, as if under her window. She waited and waited in breathless silence and expectation, listening eagerly, assured she was not deceiving herself, and that there was somebody trying to get into the house.

She felt disposed to call Norah, but second thought told her Norah was nervous, and would cry out and alarm them. She crept out of bed, and put her feet into her soft slippers, and wondered what was best to do. Then she remembered to have heard the other day of a robbery at a house no great distance from The Ridgway, and that the thieves had got safely away with their booty. What could Bates be doing? Was it possible that he could be assisting them in any way? If she only dared show herself in white, that might frighten them, perhaps; thieves were always cowards, she knew. But then she did not want to frighten them, but to have them secured, if possible. She crept to the door of her room, and gently drew it open. The extreme stillness of the house made her feel almost nervous, and her heart beat quickly and loudly. She looked, and saw a faint streak of light from under the door almost opposite.

She made one or two steps forward into the
hall, when, to her intense surprise, she saw distinctly a dark figure coming towards her—a
man—a thief—a robber. Oh, heavens! She
could not move or speak. The man carried
something in his arms, and he also came to
a stand-still, and did not speak. A deep sigh,
which Kate made in her effort to articu-
late, caused the man to start and drop what
he held out of his arms—it was the silver
commonly in use from the pantry. The crash
gave Kate courage, and, without moving a
step, and putting out her hand, she said, in
a deep low voice, "What are you doing
here?" The man gave one bound past her,
towards the dining-room door; but quick
as lightning she darted forward, held him
by his coat and hair, and screamed loudly,
"Fire! murder! murder!" In much less
time than it takes to write this, Norah and
Bates had come to Kate's assistance. Bates
had heard the fall of the silver, and struck a

light; immediately hearing Kate's screams,
he had come, just as he was, to the rescue.
Then Mrs. and Miss Leigh, and Miss
Casteldi, with the other servants, came
down, half awake and terribly frightened;
and when the former fully realized the
danger Kate had been in, they were quite
overcome, and could scarcely believe she
was not at all hurt. The coachman was
sent for from the Lodge, and, with Bates,
guarded the prisoner till he was willingly
resigned to the tender care and protection
of the village constable. That worthy
person seemed to regret deeply that he had
not had the pleasure of catching the aforesaid individual.

It turned out in the evidence that Bates
had been in to the county town on business for his mistress that evening, and at
the public-house where he refreshed himself
and horse, he had got into conversation with
two respectable men, and drank with them.

"They must have drugged the beer," he said; for he assured Mr. Clenning, who was a magistrate, and came over to The Ridgway the next day, "that his head was fit to burst, and he felt quite ill, although he had taken very little."

The thief made a clean breast of it, and did not attempt to hide who his accomplices were, so that there was no difficulty in bringing them all into the hands of justice, to receive the reward of their labours; and the man who struggled with Kate, openly expressed his admiration of Kate's "pluck," as he called it, and his sorrow for his misdeeds. The most absurd stories got about as to the injuries Kate had received. Some said her eyes were black and her wrists broken; others had even more exaggerated accounts to tell; and no one would believe that no harm had happened to her. Of course they had to delay their departure for a few days, and her time was thoroughly taken up with seeing people who came from far and near, and telling just how it happened.

"My darling," said Lord Denton, "how I long to horsewhip the wretch. Are you perfectly certain he did not strike you?"

"Oh, quite positive," replied Kate, smiling. " I do not need your pity one-half so much as the poor man does; for, oh! how I clutched at his hair, to be sure! I must have pulled handfuls out, I think."

"I doubt that," replied her lover, taking hold of her hand, and putting his own beside it, smiling at the contrast in size and colour. "Now if *this* had clutched, as you say, Kate,"—holding up his own hand, —"he might have just been able to feel the difference."

Poor Mrs. Clenning was more put out than any one else. She was quite overcome with the idea of such dreadful practices going on so near them. She positively

declared she would never have another
moment's peace of mind till "something"
was done to prevent the possibility of anything of the kind happening at the Hall,
as it would surely be the death of her
if she even heard a robber in the house.
What that "something" was, Mrs. Clenning
never clearly understood herself, nor ex-
plained to any of her family; but after
awhile the whole affair was forgotten, or at
least less talked about, and Mrs. Clenning
regained her small share of confidence and
feeling of security, and ceased to anticipate
the being put to death by violent hands
in her own house, or dying from fear of
such a sad calamity.

CHAPTER VIII.

"MAMMA," said Helen Leigh, "what an eventful time we have had of it since Kate has been with us! I can scarcely believe that she has gone, and that we are to fall back again into the old quiet groove."

"You are right, Helen, we have. I certainly feel as if all the commotion had been too much for me. I am half inclined to go away for a few weeks' entire rest and change. We should both be the better for it, I think, for you have not looked at all like yourself for some time past," said Mrs. Leigh.

"Oh, mamma, love, I am really quite

well; but a change is just the thing. I should like it so much, and shall be able to do all the more work when I come back, and you are always the better for going away."

"Then, Helen, we will decide to go very soon; and I tell you another thing that occurred to me this morning—we might, perhaps, persuade Mrs. Clayton to come with us as our guest for at least part of the time, and the vicar could join us now and then, if we do not go too far away."

"Well, mother, this is kind of you, in-deed. You are always doing others good just when they want it most. I hope they may have no scruples about accepting your hospitality away from home. I know they are very self-denying, but I don't think they can easily refuse to go in that way with us."

"I will call to-day, Helen, as I go into town, and do my best to ask them in a way

which will show them it will be a favour to
us if they consent to join us."

.Mr. and Mrs. Clayton had one son, who
had been a constant source of anxiety and
trouble to them. Though their grief was
too great to talk of, Mrs. Leigh knew that
through his misdeeds they had so many calls
upon their limited, narrow purse, that it
was almost impossible for them to afford a
jaunt of any kind for pleasure, and for some
time both husband and wife had been falling
off sadly in health; and it was thinking of
all this that had put the suggestion to her
really kind and thoughtful heart of the little
plan she had mentioned to her daughter.

She got to the Vicarage too late for anything but a hurried visit, as she left it till
she returned from town; but she carried
back to Helen the good news that Mr. and
Mrs. Clayton were both very pleased to accept
her offer. So they all went off the following week to C——; and as the weather

was fine and warm, they were out of doors on the sea-shore almost all day. Mr. Clayton returned for his Sunday duties, but joined them again on the Monday or Tuesday. Helen had always been a great favourite with the vicar. He frequently said she was as much help as a curate would have been, and that he would have to give up working if she went away.

"I am so glad you think me really useful to you, Mr. Clayton," Helen said one day when he had returned, bringing all sorts of messages for her from home. "It is so pleasant to feel that one can do something for others, even though that may be very little."

"You are quite right, Helen," replied her friend; "and you must also bear in mind always that some of us 'must be content to fill a little space.' It is not always in the widest sphere of work that the greatest good is done. It is not the amount of work we do, but the motives which prompt us to do it, and the way we do it in, which should guide us constantly. Don't get discontented, Helen, because you work unseen."

"Oh, no, surely not, Mr. Clayton; why should I? If I have made you think I am discontented at any time, I can assure you now truly that I am not. On the contrary, I am thankful for all my blessings, I hope and trust; but you know one hears so much of what women are doing now-a-days, working so hard and doing so much, that perhaps I fancy sometimes I might strike out, as it were, and do a good deal more to help others than I have yet done."

"Ah, well, Helen, it is generally allowed that all women can 'talk' well; whether they 'work' well, is a totally different thing," said Mr. Clayton. "But it strikes me very forcibly that there is too much talking going on now, and that women are gradually losing their love of, and their claim to, the gentler and holier duties of life. Of course I am old-fashioned, and out of the world; I know so little of what is going on, except from hearsay, and perhaps ought not to give my opinion so freely; but as far as you are concerned, Helen, you may be pretty sure you are filling the place Providence has portioned out for you. 'Inasmuch as ye have done it unto these my brethren, ye have done it unto me.'"

Helen often managed to have a little confidential chat with Mr. Clayton. He was so much like a father to her, and so interested in all she did, that she was very much at ease with him, and took him into her confidence quite freely.

"Mamma," exclaimed Annie Clenning, "here is a letter from Miss Byrne She asks if Julia and Mary and I will be her bridesmaids. The wedding is to take place early in the new year, she says; and we are to go over a few days before, to see about any alterations in the dresses. Isn't it delightful for us all, mamma?"

"Why, Annie, there is plenty of time between this and then for her to change her mind twenty times. She is just the kind of girl to do so, I fancy; so don't make up your mind too positively," said Mrs. Clenning.

"Oh, no, mamma; please don't say so," replied Annie. "Miss Byrne is not changeable. Whatever other failings she may have, I don't think that can be laid to her charge; on the contrary, she always carries out anything she takes into her head, Helen says."

"Then of course Helen knows her better than I do; but at any rate there is plenty of time to think about it, though indeed you must let her know you accept the offer as soon as possible. But weddings are not always pleasant, Annie; indeed, I may say scarcely ever. I can assure you, the day I was married to your papa, my poor mamma and I cried as if our hearts would break, and so did my bridesmaids too, until I went away in the afternoon; so my memory brings back to me no delightful remembrances."

"Well, I promise you, mamma, that if ever I am married, I will try not to shed a single tear, and will bind all my friends over to follow my example, just for a treat and change to you," said Annie, gaily.

Mrs. Clenning forced a smile,—a very melancholy one, it is true,—and dictated a reply to Miss Byrne, thanking her for thinking of her daughters, and for her kind inquiries after them all. Her own health, she assured Kate, was as wretchedly bad as ever; but she hoped, if she was spared, that she would soon have the pleasure of welcoming Kate to Denton Court.

Mr. and Mrs. Clayton, Helen and her

mother, all came back from their sea-side
outing very much the better for it. Helen
looked less pale and thin, and Mrs. Clayton
was certainly greatly improved. Kate had
written long letters to Helen, telling her
all her plans, and asking Mrs. Leigh to be
kind enough to give Lord Denton the benefit
of any suggestion she might have about the
alterations that were to take place at his
house. "He will come to see you soon,"
she added; "and perhaps you will drive
over with him, and take a look at the rooms,
and see what needs to be done. I am going
to be so unusually busy, that I shall have
very little time for anything but my preparations, as it flies so quickly."

Did Kate during these busy weeks ever
let her thoughts go back to the early part
of the year, when one who was far away
from her now had been her almost constant
companion? Did she ever think of their
walks, rides, and chats? Did she ever

wonder if he thought of her, and where and how she was? Did the "still, small voice" within (which we all hear sometimes, and must listen to) ever suggest to her what might have been—what, perhaps, ought to have been—if she had only been true to him and herself? Did she ever wonder if her future would be as happy with the man she had freely chosen, as it might have been with the one she had so carelessly thrown aside? If any of these thoughts did occur, they did not remain to trouble her; she was little given to reflection of any kind, and particularly disliked dwelling on the past, especially if it was not pleasant.

Lord Denton stayed some weeks in Ireland, making acquaintance with Kate's relations and friends. On all sides he heard praises of his lady-love's beauty, talents, generosity, and good-nature; and when he saw how very much she was admired and sought after, he could but agree with those

who told him that he was one of the most
fortunate individuals in existence to have
gained the heart and hand of so lovely a
woman, and one so well fitted to shine in
society and receive homage from every one.
It is just possible that women of that kind
are not those peculiarly adapted to make
happy homes; but then we cannot combine
beauty of soul and mind with the beauty
of outward form as easily as we might wish,
so that if we take the one we must be content to do without the other.

It is not to be supposed that Lord Denton
had any of these ideas. Men in love seldom
moralize: they generally give themselves up
to the full enjoyment of the delightful feeling
which throws all others into the background
for at least a time, and hardly ever pause to
consider any questions of the wisdom of the
course they intend to take. He was not, however, quite satisfied with Kate's manner to
him; she kept him so far from her, and seemed

so little inclined to be alone with him, or allow any of the tender endearments which he longed to show her as proofs of his love, that he did sometimes wonder if she really cared for him. Then, perhaps, a smile from her, or a request put in her most winning fashion, would dispel all doubt, and he willingly went on, submitting to the usual small tyrannies which women generally exercise over men they know to be really deeply in love with them; and he felt every day more anxious for the time to come which would make her his for ever, and set aside all restraint between them. He returned to S——shire full of plans for restoring and beautifying Denton Court, and making it fit for the reception of its future mistress. Rooms that for years had scarcely seen the light of day were to be swept and garnished; old-fashioned furniture was to be put aside, or done away with altogether, to be replaced by modern elegant additions and substitutes, and no expense was to be spared which could add to its comfort or improvement.

"Why, mamma," said Helen, after a visit of Lord Denton to them, "I can scarcely believe he is the same man, the last few months have worked such changes in him. He might be a youth of one or two and twenty, he seems so undecided and puzzled as to Kate's choice of things."

"It is certainly the first time I have known or heard of his being interested in anything, Helen, at all useful, and I begin to think we have all been mistaken about him," added Mrs. Leigh.

"How amused Kate would be if she knew the trouble he has taken before deciding what the colour should be in the reception-rooms. As to Kate's own boudoir, it will be a lovely little snuggery. I quite long to see her there," said Helen.

"But that is Kate's own wish to have

fawn and green satin there. Lord Denton told me she had chosen her own colours for her own rooms," replied Mrs. Leigh.

" I am glad of that, mamma, because she is very particular about light shades, I know; and though I admired the pattern he chose, I did fancy it ought to have been sent to Kate before it was decided on."

Mrs. Leigh and her daughter were very much interested in all that went on. Kate was so dear to both of them, that they almost felt as if they were assisting at preparations for some one belonging to them. The workmen put the old place in too great a muddle for Lord Denton to remain with any comfort; so he ran up to London, and came down occasionally to see how matters were progressing. The winter set in early with unusual severity, and merry Christmas was something like an old-fashioned one, with its frosts and snows. Kate's maiden days were rapidly drawing to an end, and every

moment of her time was fully occupied with
the hundreds of little worrying items that
the preparing for a fashionable· marriage
of necessity entails. Helen left home on
New-Year's-Eve very reluctantly without her
mother; but, as some of her relations were
on a visit to her, Mrs. Leigh could not very
well leave them, and was really glad of so good
an excuse for not taking a long journey in
such severe weather. Lord Denton followed
her a day or two later with the Misses
Clenning and their brother; and poor Julia
arrived more like a ghost than a living being,
the short passage from Holyhead to Kings-
town having been exceedingly rough, and
nearly two hours longer than usual. They
were all three glad to retire to rest, but
Annie and Mary had been frivolous and
eager to look over all the beautiful presents
and things of the bride, as well as their own
lockets, which had come home that day.
They were handsome enough to satisfy even

Annie's fastidious taste, had the initial letters of Kate and Lord Denton as a monogram in pearls and emeralds, and, after trying her own on the former young person, she pronounced them "perfectly lovely."

The settlements were all drawn up, after the delays customary in such matters; everything had been done to everybody's satisfaction. Lord Denton having made a handsome sum over entirely for Kate's use, her own money was settled upon herself, so that, under any circumstances, she would always be thoroughly well supplied with money. Helen had not ventured to make any inquisitive questions, although she had been altogether with Kate; but she was so happy and sanguine, and seemed so thoroughly at ease, entering into everything with so much zest and enjoyment,— nothing seeming to give her any trouble,— that it was impossible for Helen not to feel that, after all, perhaps Kate never had loved

Bartle, and that she was entering upon her new life with every appearance of reciprocal love and confidence. The night before the wedding came at last; there was a great trying on of dresses of those bridesmaids who were staying in the house, and when nothing remained to be done, they all went to their rooms.

"Good night, Nellie. Don't come in; I would rather be alone to-night, dear," said Kate, as Helen passed her room. "I shall be so thankful when to-morrow is over." She was quite tired, and hurried Norah over her duties, and out of the room, much to the surprise of the faithful handmaid, who was generally very necessary to her young mistress's evening toilette, and often indulged with little pleasant conversations about every-day events. But to-night, of all nights, when there was so much to be talked over, it was rather hard not to be allowed to say a cheep, and to find the door locked upon

her. Kate made no attempt to retire to
rest; she sat at the fire with a book, her
toes on the fender, carelessly turning over
and glancing at the pages. Then she laid
the book on her lap, and, resting her head on
her hand, looked steadily and thoughtfully
into the fire. Whether the past or future
occupied her most, we cannot attempt to say.
Certain it is that some long time passed
without her moving, and that two or three
hot tears, which dropped on the hand
which held the book on her lap, made her
start up quickly. It was so very rarely she
shed tears, that she was almost surprised at
herself, and brushing them hastily away,
as if ashamed of her weakness, she exclaimed,—" Dear, good, loving father, no
one will ever understand me as well as you
have,"—she threw herself on her knees by
the side of the bed, and prayed earnestly for
help and guidance in the unknown future.
It was no use for her now to try to dash her

tears away or stop them, to call herself weak
and foolish; they flowed freely, full, and hot,
as she bent her head over her bed. Whether
her prayer had made her give way, and
softened her thoughts, or whether the trying
and solemn ceremony which she had to go
through the next day may have presented
itself to her in a different light, and caused
this burst of better feeling, it is hard to say;
but undoubtedly Kate Byrne was more sad
and subdued that night than she had ever
been before in all her life.

CHAPTER IX.

THE wedding was to take place at ten o'clock, so that all the household were astir very early. Kate did not leave her room, nor would she admit any of her young friends who offered their assistance but Helen, who came directly after breakfast to help in giving the finishing touches, and found Miss Casteldi already there, taking a quiet cup of coffee with Kate.

"How cold your hands are, Kitty, love; like bits of ice, I declare. Do warm them before you finish your dressing."

"It is not tropical weather just now, Nellie, you will allow. I would rather be cold than hot: one can never do anything

well if one is heated. So don't bother me,
please, auntie," she said, as she waved away
the offer of a chair that her aunt wanted her
to sit in before the fire.

"There, Kate," exclaimed Helen, when
the bridal wreath was fastened, "you grand,
glorious creature, how splendid you look,
—fit bride for a king. How I wish mamma
could see you at this moment. Give me a
kiss, love, for I must away and finish my
own dressing"; and, placing her arms round
Kate, she gave her an earnest, loving em-
brace, with her eyes full of happy tears.

"Now, Helen, don't be a goose, please,"
said Kate, quickly. "I cannot endure anything of the kind to-day. You know I hate
scenes at any time, so remember that if you
can, and oblige me by not following the
usual bridesmaid's fashion of spoiling your
eyes and complexion. Now all of you go,
please, and let papa fetch me when my
carriage comes."

As Mr. Byrne led his lovely child down the aisle he trembled, but she walked proudly by his side, white as the snowy lace and satin she was dressed in; and on all sides there were exclamations of delight and satisfaction at the elegant appearance of the whole party.

Lord Denton had been waiting impatiently in the vestry, as nervous and flurried as most men are upon such occasions; and he certainly presented a striking contrast, with his full, flushed face, to the pale tall girl at his side. As the minister read the service slowly and impressively, Kate never raised her eyes from the altar step; but she made her replies in a firm low voice which was distinctly heard by all around her. Then she knelt beside the man she had vowed to love and honour all the days of her life, and received the blessing of her pastor and friend. They were all full of fun and congratulatory complimenting in the vestry while the register was being signed; then they made way for the bride and bridegroom to pass out through the bevy of smiling fair faces. Many were the blessings breathed for them both as they passed to their carriage, closely followed by the admiring crowd who had gathered to see the wedding. As soon as they moved away from the church, Lord Denton drew down the blinds, not to keep out the sunshine, for there had been none that morning, but to place his arms around her, and say, "My precious wife, my own for ever."

There was no time to be lost at the breakfast, as the boat started early, which gave Kate an excuse for hurrying from the table. Norah had everything ready to re-deck her child, as she always called Kate, so that the change was soon made, and the last good-byes said. "Come here, Kitty, just a moment," said Mr. Byrne; and she went into the hall. He drew her into his own room, and held her in his arms, kissing her pale cheek and lips, and blessing her again and again. "God bless you, darling," was all he could say. A few moments later the carriage was off, a shower of satin shoes following in various directions after it; and Mr. Byrne felt that the gap made in his heart and home could never be filled. A crowd of small boys had lingered about the house to see them go away. They were not over-well clad or very clean. They looked sad, hungry, and cold, so Kate insisted upon her husband throwing a good handful of silver out of the carriage window to them, to the great delight of them all. There was a pretty good struggle for each to get a share, and a lingering and hunting after any stray coin that might have chanced to have escaped notice; but each one got something, and went away in much better spirits, to tell his good fortune to his friends.

There was a large, crowded assembly at
Mr. Byrne's in the evening. The young
people danced and flirted, while their elders
amused themselves with less fatiguing pleasures. The Irishmen on this occasion did
full justice to their " national characteristic."
Of course, they may have paid a visit to
the celebrated castle near Killarney, and
" kissed the Blarney Stone on the top of
its wall," for the express purpose of making
themselves irresistible to the English girls
on this particular evening; but whether or
no, the ladies voted them one and all de-
lightfully pleasant and agreeable. Helen
and the Misses Clemming stayed a few
days with Mr. Byrne and Miss Casteldi,
Julia dreading to cross again till the sea
was a trifle calmer. When they returned
home in high spirits, they did nothing for
days but talk and tell of all the delightful
times they had had, and even made their
mother almost believe that a wedding is

not always quite such a miserable ceremony as she fancied. They also tried to persuade their father to take them for a tour in Ireland, for they had heard so much of the beauties to be seen there that they quite longed to go again with him. However, an event which happened soon after this gave a fresh turn to their plans and wishes: for Mary's pretty little face and figure had captivated the heart of a certain Captain Mylett, who found that he was too frequently thinking of her to be at all up to his usual duties; and as young Clenning had invited him to come to see them if he was ever in their neighbourhood, he made a point of going there by way of a change, visited them, and when he went away he was Mary's accepted lover. They were married after a very short engagement, and Julia and Annie often paid pleasant visits to the west of Ireland, where the newly-married pair took up their abode.

Helen gave her mother and her friends the Claytons so minute a description of everything, that they could scarcely have known more if they had been eye-witnesses. Mr. Byrne would fain have kept Helen with him some months, for he thought he should never reconcile himself to the quiet and loneliness of the house without his child; but of course Helen's own mother could ill spare her, for her health was changeable, and her home lonely too, especially as her visitors had gone away. Mr. Byrne told Helen to tell her mother "that he had serious thoughts of letting his house and coming to England to live, to be nearer his daughter. He had talked the matter over with Miss Casteldi, and, as far as she was concerned, she would like him to do so; but, at the same time, perhaps, as far as the Dentons were to be considered, it would be a greater treat for them to come over to Blackrock, especially as Kate was so fond of the old place."

"Wouldn't it be a pity, mamma, to let it,—it is such a nice place, and the house so elegantly furnished? Then Mr. Byrne knows everybody far and near, and the climate suits him, too. Of course, he will get more reconciled if he waits a little. It is too late in life for him to begin to make fresh friends in a strange place; don't you think so, mamma?"

"Oh, yes, certainly I do, Helen," replied Mrs. Leigh. "It will require a good deal of consideration before he decides to leave it, I dare say. I can though quite understand the feeling which prompts the idea, for I fear, Helen, I should be very much tempted to follow you if you went away from me."

Helen reddened, and assured her mother that she had no intention of ever leaving her. She was too happy at home to be

sufficiently satisfied with any other kind of
life or duties, or to be induced to make a
change to please anybody.

⸱After spending a few days at a country
place of one of his friends in the south of
England, Lord Denton took his bride to
Paris, intending to go farther on, to any
place that either might take a fancy to see.
The weather was cold and frosty, but bright
and clear, and enjoyable. Whatever con-
fessions he may have had to make to her,
he had not yet found a good opportunity of
taking her into his confidence. In fact, if
the truth were told, he had begun to fancy
that, perhaps, as they were now really
married, and nothing could or ought to
come between them, he need not trouble her
with them. He was so doubtful as to how she
would look upon the affair, that he was
anxious not to make her the least angry or
annoyed with him. Then he thought he
would write in confidence to her father and

explain the matter; but then, again, he knew
he ought to have at least mentioned it to
him when he proposed to him, or rather
to Kate. But he had not done so, and now
—as is always the case with every one if
they delay to do what is right—it seemed
almost impossible to refer to it either to his
wife or her father; so perhaps, after all, it
was best not to think any more about it,
but keep it, as he had always done, sacred,
and ten chances to one no word of it would
ever come to their ears.

Lord Denton, it will be seen, had very
little decision of character or courage. He
was kind-hearted and generous, and anxious
to do right and please others, but he had
no control over his actions. It was almost
impossible for him to say no to any one;
he was as easily led as a little child, and
often, in spite of himself, did what he afterwards regretted, merely because some one
had persuaded him, or made him believe

that it was all right, and would oblige them.

They were staying at one of the hotels in the Rue de Rivoli, and their windows looked out into the Gardens of the Tuileries, at one of which Kate seated herself one afternoon after coming in from her drive. She did not look particularly happy; she had, in fact, been disappointed about some home letters which she quite expected in the morning, and had wondered and fretted about them, fearing her papa or aunt might be ill. She was gazing out into the fast-coming twilight when her husband joined her and sat down by her side, and placed his arm round her waist.

"What is my peerless Kitty thinking so deeply about, that she did not even turn to see who it was when I came into the room?"

"Oh, I knew it was you, therefore I had no occasion to turn round to look," replied

Kate; "and I was thinking how much dear papa is missing me."

"Of course he does, darling; but you don't regret leaving him, do you, love? Tell me truly," said her husband.

"Well, I scarcely know if I do or not; of course not in one sense of the word; but you surely do not object to my thinking of him sometimes? You would not have me forget him, I suppose?"

"Forget him, Kate; how you misunderstand me, to be sure!" exclaimed Denton. "Why, I wouldn't take one simple, happy thought from you under any circumstances, my darling. You looked a little sad, I thought, and that made me ask you."

"Well, but don't begin to fidget about my looks," replied Kate, smiling. "I can't help my face being an expressive one, nor can I help thinking sometimes, and being a trifle subdued; but I promise to tell you, if I am ever unhappy enough to wish for

sympathy, though I assure you I don't anticipate anything of the kind."

"I have a good deal to tell you though,
Kate, indeed, which I should have told you
some time ago; but our days went on so
quickly that I never liked to waste them;
and besides, now you are really all my
own, I shall hope for forgiveness with
more confidence than I should have had
then."

"Oh, dreadful!" said Kate, holding up
her hands in seeming horror. "I do hope I
am not to hear you have committed some
awful crime, the secret of which you expect
me to burden my conscience with for ever,
in proof of the obedience I so lately promised you. I must beg to be excused, if
such is the case, for I hate secrets and scenes
particularly, and cannot keep the former;
besides, the walls have ears, and we may
be pounced upon by some violent member
of the police here, and carried off to prison."

"Now, Kate, do be serious just for half an hour, and listen to me. You know, darling, you will soon be hearing my own friends' opinions of my unworthy self, and it is just possible that some one may—"

The door opened suddenly, and a servant came in with a tray and letters. Kate bounded up and snatched them all off. "Ah, here is one from dear papa, George. I am glad, dear darling," she exclaimed, as she kissed the envelope and tore it open, devouring the contents.

"Delightful! how good of him! He is really coming to meet us in London when we return, if all is well, and Aunt Neta too. Isn't it nice, George? There are plenty of loving messages for both of us; and he ends by hoping that we are as happy as the days are long. He couldn't have remembered that they happen just now to be uncommonly short, could he, do you think? Do read it for yourself. I am so happy to have received it; and please ring for lights, for me to see what my other friends say."

The lights came, and Lord Denton felt very indisposed to touch the letter held out to him. She had shown so little interest in his affairs, and appeared to have entirely forgotten that he had anything to say. It was like adding insult to injury; but as he caught sight of his wife's animated face, he could not resist it. So he took the letter and read it, Kate leaning and looking over his shoulder the while. Why did not some good angel prompt Kate, when her husband had finished reading, and they had talked the contents over, to ask him to go on with what he had to say? How much doubt and fear it would have spared her in after years! So far from mentioning it, she never even thought of it. They were going to a reception in the evening, and wanted to be early; so that, what with dressing for dinner, and then again later, it did not enter her busy head, and Lord Denton never again made the slightest allusion to it. He was so justly proud of her that night; and, as he saw her at a distance in close conversation with a French nobleman, he comforted himself with the assurance that, of all women in the world, perhaps Kate was the least likely for any living being to presume to broach unpleasant things to. A glance of her eye, or a curl of that short upper lip, was enough, or more than enough, to silence or prevent any piece of impertinence, however intimate she might become with any of his old acquaintances. So he must trust to time and "luck" to hide the past, and make the future as agreeable as earthly mortals could possibly hope for.

"Mamma, here is a letter from Kate. They are at Nice, it appears. I quite thought they intended going on to Rome, but they have changed their minds, apparently, and are going no farther south, as far as I can make out. But I will read it aloud," said Helen; "at least all that will interest you, mamma.

" ' The decree has gone forth, my dear Helen, that "so far we shall go, and no farther"; and whether we shall overstep the bounds we have given ourselves or no, I cannot say; don't be surprised, however, to hear of us from anywhere, for somehow I cannot stay long in any place just now, and we may come home very soon. I had a delightful time in Paris; it was very cold, and I had plenty of use for my furs, which were handsomer than any one else's that I saw. This place is very full. We are staying at one of the villa hotels behind the town, beautifully situate among the gardens and olive woods. How I wish you were here, Nellie; in fact, I have wished for you continually. Perhaps it is not quite the thing to say in one's honeymoon, but I certainly think that if two people are

too much together, they feel each other a
bore. But independent of that, I am sure
you would enjoy being here so much. Not
having the pen of a ready writer, I can't
attempt to describe the place. I can only
say I like it better than most places I have
been to; it is sunny and warm, and, if it
were not for the white dust, which covers
everything and everybody, it would be quite
perfect. There is a delightful, nice, open
drive, with a walk all along the beach, quite
two miles long, which ends towards the town
in a square, shady garden, with hotels all
round; and this is crowded every afternoon
with loungers from every quarter of the
globe, I should fancy, dressed in the most
brilliant costumes, seated in chairs, between
which those who prefer walking promenade, stare, quiz, and meet their friends
and acquaintances. There are a great
number of slovenly, though richly dressed
Americans here now; some Russians, and

plenty of English—a great many of whom
are more or less delicate, I dare say. The
Earl of M—— is here, and his delicate,
pretty daughter, quite a shadow, and so
patient. George introduced me, and she
begged me to call on her, which I did yesterday. It was so pleasant to talk to her. She
knows she is in a critical condition, and
is quite prepared not to get better. I think
her rather like you, Nellie, in face, and
manner too, a little; so that is why I have
taken such a fancy to her, perhaps. Then
the Gilberts are here, all of them, and their
friends, Lord and Lady P——, and children,
whom we meet every day, and with whom
we exchange greetings. A pretty, tiny girl
(American) is staying at our hotel, with her
father (an unusual occurrence, I find, as they
generally prefer the larger and handsomer
ones), and the contrast between them is so
great that I am amused with it. She is quite
a child in appearance, not more, I am sure,

than four feet six or seven inches high, but
so pretty, and constantly talking and lolling
about in the most lackadaisical fashion, order-
ing her numerous admirers about here and
there, and asking for her "pa," as she calls
him, constantly. I am, be it known, under
the ban of her displeasure; for *why* I
cannot tell, except that, perhaps, I have
looked at her once or twice when I have
heard her talking and calling out, and my
looks may have been too severe for her.
Her father is devoted to her, but certainly
in all my life I never met any one at
all like him,—tall and gaunt, excessively
miserable-looking, with the coarsest manner
I ever heard of. However, this is scandal,
and you won't care a jot for it, I know.
So I will go on to tell you that there is a
capital band and plenty of balls and concerts at the Casino; also gambling in a
quiet sort of way, I believe, though of
course, as the Government professes to hold

it illegal, there is little said about it. Then a small steamer takes a fair share of the visitors to Monaco, where there is a regular table, and many people come to Nice for no other reason than its close proximity to Monaco. Don't suppose that because I tell you all this, Nellie, I am going to commence gambling. My love of card-playing has not diminished, I own; but still it will not lead me on yet, I hope, to any deeper play. It is one of the things I intend to reserve for old or middle age; so tell your mamma, with my love, that she need have no fears about me. Write to me by return, please Helen, and tell me all about everybody and everything. I so long to see you all again. Papa intends to meet us in London, and stay with us till we come to Denton, at the end of the summer. I must say good-bye now, for if I wrote pages I should not say what I really want; so will make up for all when I see you. Love to your dear mamma, and remembrances to all inquiring friends.'

" There, mamma, that is all. I wish she had said more about herself. She scarcely mentions her husband either, or asks a question about the house," said Helen, as she folded up the letter.

" You know very well, Helen love, that Kate never wrote a satisfactory letter yet; but she is no doubt as well as usual, and quite enjoying all the gaiety that comes in her way; though why they stay there, I cannot imagine."

A day or two after Kate had written to Helen, she and her husband were driving slowly along the promenade, when suddenly Lord Denton sprang forward, called to the coachman to stop, and said to Kate, " By Jove! there's Martin." Who Martin was she had not the least idea, and had no time to inquire; for Lord Denton got out of the carriage, and was among the crowd in a moment.

"Drive on," said Kate; but they had scarcely gone a few yards when her husband and his friend, Captain Martin, came to the side of the carriage, and it again stopped, and Lady Denton was introduced to him, her husband telling her that they were very old friends indeed.

"Do get in, Martin, and drive with us, and let us know what has brought you here of all places in the world. Come, get in," said Lord Denton.

"No, thank you, Denton; I can't leave Clough, you know; unless he comes too, I don't think I can," replied Martin.

"I will go and fetch him; there is plenty of room, and we may as well all go together," said Lord Denton.

"I should prefer driving on at once, if you please," said Kate; "this waiting about annoys me. There is plenty of time for you to see your friend, I should think, as he says

he is staying here, and we happen to be doing the same."

"Ah, certainly; I beg your pardon, Kitty. Well, good-bye, Martin, I will look you up to-night," said Lord Denton, as he shook hands and jumped into his seat.

Captain Martin stood aside, hat in hand, and bowed low to Kate's slight bend of the head. After watching them for a moment or two, he returned to his young friend and companion.

CHAPTER X.

IS that beautiful girl Denton's daughter, Martin?" asked Mr. Clough, as soon as his friend returned to his chair.

"Daughter! no indeed; his wife, I should say. Deuced pretty girl, no doubt; but Irish, I find, and fiery I'll wager."

"Pretty!" replied the younger man. "Why, she is the loveliest woman I've seen here, and that is saying a good deal. I saw her very well while you were talking to her, and quite envied you."

"Did you indeed? then you made a mistake. She didn't say half-a-dozen words to me, my boy, I assure you; cold and proud as Lucifer, if I may venture an opinion."

her a feeling that she could not describe to herself. Of course she saw him again and again, but, instead of wearing off, the feeling deepened, and though she was always polite, it was a frigid, distant politeness, which annoyed him terribly.

"Why shouldn't she be civil?" he asked himself again and again. "A fellow might be a toad or a serpent"—not a flattering comparison, it must be allowed.

Had Kate been asked why she disliked him, she could not have answered. There the feeling was; she could scarcely bear his being near her, and she could scarcely disguise her feelings from him. She thought of telling her husband, and of begging him not to bring his friend; but that seemed so stupid and childish, that she did not like to mention it. He was so different from the men she had been used to meet—talked freely of things which she certainly had never heard mentioned before her by any one, and repeated any scandal of the worst kind, by way of conversation, with the greatest relish and excuses for the offending person. Kate had many faults, it must be allowed, the effect of a too indulgent bringing-up. But she was quite refined and pure in all her ideas and thoughts; and the free, careless, light way in which she heard some of her own sex spoken of by her husband's friend made her shrink from him with horror. She was so surprised, too, that her husband did not notice it: he laughed, and listened, and joked, and apparently forgot it the next moment. But Kate is not the first girl, either married or single, who has been struck with this freedom of speech in some circles of the upper class: it is a painful, but true fact, and cannot be too strongly objected to by those who dislike it.

Lord Denton had noticed Kate's distaste for his friend's society, and in reality was not displeased. Of all his acquaintances,

Martin would have been the last that he would willingly have brought Kate in contact with. He knew so much more than most people did of his general character and goings-on, that he had fully intended, after his marriage, to see much less of him ; but then "chance" had thrown them together now, and it would certainly be pleasanter for all of them if Kate was not quite so frigid. He was really a good-natured, jolly sort of fellow with all his faults, and it would be too bad to cut him just for a freak of Kate's fancy. So they saw a good deal of each other every day for a week, and Kate was left alone, which made her make up her mind to return as soon as possible to London. Late one evening, when her husband returned more flushed and heated than usual, she asked him where he had been, and why he stayed so late.

"Oh, only with Martin and Clough, darling," he replied, coming and trying to take hold of her waist. "You know I told you not to expect me early; the boat was so crowded and late. I hope you have not been anxious?"

"Not the least, indeed, but I dislike being left hours and hours alone here. You seem to forget *I* have no friends; if I had, you may be certain I should not trouble myself to remonstrate with you, if you chose to pass every moment of the day with yours," replied Kate, moving away from him.

"I am so truly sorry, Kitty; no wonder you are cross, brute that I have been; but it won't happen again, love, I assure you, as I don't intend to go to Monaco any more."

"You may go exactly where you please with your charming friends. I should though have given you credit for a little better taste, at least, than you have shown in the selection of those two contemptible creatures," replied Kate, angrily.

"Now, Kate, you are too hard upon them.

Clough is a little foppish, I grant, and Martin is not handsome, but he can't help that, and the nicest fellow I know."

" Is he indeed?" interrupted Kate. "Then, if you have no better specimen of what a gentleman is than ' Martin,' as you call him, I think it is a great pity I did not see your friends before I married you."

" Just let me finish, Kate. I was going to add, only you catch me up so quickly, that I have known him so long and so intimately, that I am sorry to see him out of sorts. He has a wretched cough, and is in dreadfully low spirits about himself, so of course I try to cheer him up a bit for old ' lang syne.' "

" I have not a word more to say about the matter, but I certainly wish to go from here at once. If no other place is ready, I can go to papa and take Norah; you can stay and comfort your friend."

Lord Denton saw that Kate was too angry to be persuaded out of her present state of mind, and knew it was no use following her from the room, so he lighted his cigar and mentally exclaimed against his own stupidity, called himself all the brutes and fools he could think of for leaving her so long by herself. No wonder she was angry and wanted to go home. He must try, however, to prevent her doing that; if she only thought over it a moment she would see how absurd the idea was. He wished from his heart that Martin had not turned up then; it was quite impossible to resist him when they were together. And to think that their first difference should be through him, it was very vexing; but Kate would be all sunshine again in the morning, he trusted, and then, if she would leave Nice, he should suggest their going to Rome or Venice. The next morning, at breakfast, Kate asked him quite quietly if he had thought over what she had said the evening before.

"I do not particularly wish to rush to

England, but I wish to go from here. I am
tired of it and dull, nor can I be happy if I
stay. I tire soon of places, I must confess,
and I fear I may add the weakness soon of
taking the same feeling as to people, which
would be most unpleasant sometimes, I dare
say." She looked at him in a very unpleasant, pointed manner, as she said the last
part of her sentence.

" I don't know what you mean, Kitty, in the
least," replied her husband; " but I thought
we had arranged to stay till the end of the
month. It seems so foolish to run away in
such a hurry, darling."

" Not at all," replied Kate; " and if it is,
who cares? I certainly do not; but, as I said
before, there is no occasion for you to tear
yourself away. *I* shall go,—that is, of course,
if you do not oblige me to remain."

She rose from the table having scarcely
touched anything but her coffee, and was
going out of the room, when her husband

caught hold of her and held the door, and used his best endeavours to make her give way. But Kate was firm, and declared she really meant every word she said, so at last he promised to take her away the day after. Not that he cared two straws about it beyond the wishing to keep some engagements he had made for the following week. He knew Martin would be vexed, too, and banter him well about his loss of liberty and being tied to apron-strings. And how easily Kate was vexed about trifles: it was babyish of her; and how could he refuse to do anything she wished when he loved her so very dearly? He would have given almost anything if he had not been so senseless yesterday, and caused this bother. While Kate was giving Norah directions about her packing, Lord Denton made a call upon the Captain, who had just come down in dressing-gown and slippers, looking more like a ghost than his former self.

"Glad to see you, my boy," he exclaimed, as he grasped Lord Denton's hand. "I am awfully shakey this morning—no rest for this confounded cough."

During their conversation his Lordship mentioned that they had altered their plans, and were going on to Rome for a few weeks on the morrow.

"What a confounded nuisance! Ah! I see how it is, quite at my lady's beck and call, and afraid for dear life to say your soul is your own, old boy, eh?"

"Come, come! Martin, take care! you are on dangerous ground, remember. I can't allow my *wife* to be spoken of in that manner, so in future let it be understood that it is a forbidden subject between us, if you please."

Never before had Lord Denton spoken to the Captain in such a decided tone. He had just sufficient common-sense or cunning to see that it was wisest not to reply, so he dashed off a glass of soda and brandy, apo-

logized for what he had said, and no more
notice was taken of their going away.

He told his grievance to his young friend
when he joined him, and complained in not
over-polite terms of Lady Denton's coldness
and influence over her husband. Mr. Clough,
who was not quite so disconcerted at Lady
Denton's behaviour, ventured to hope that
the Captain would soon regain his temper and
see things in a different light. They both
called at the hotel just as the Dentons were
starting, to say good-bye.

" I'm awfully sorry you are going, but I
shall look you up at the Court by-and-by, if
we don't see each other in town," exclaimed
the Captain at the last moment. " I will let
you know when I leave here."

Kate was really very grateful to her husband for yielding to her wishes, and showed
by the pleasure she took in everything they
saw at Rome that she was so. From there
they next stopped at Paris for a few days'

rest, as they had had a fatiguing journey, and Kate did not wish to get to London till her father and aunt were there to receive them. One evening, before dinner, Lord Denton came in, bringing a case of jewels in his hand, which he gave to Kate, asking her to see if she liked them.

" Ah, what darlings! they are beautiful; and how good of you to buy them for me! I could almost promise to love you for ever, they are so pretty," she said, as she turned round, holding out her arm for him to fasten the bracelet; then putting in her earrings and brooch, she went to the glass to admire them again.

Lord Denton kissed her, and replied, gravely,—

" Not surely for *them*, Kate; I trust you will love me always in spite of decorations. I will do anything you wish, my darling, to prove my love for you, and you can mould me to almost perfection, I trust, if you like."

"That is far more than I would attempt, George, for any one. A perfect man or woman would be almost worse than a very wicked one to me, I think; however, I dare say we shall both be upon our best behaviour, and manage to make a respectable appearance to our friends," replied Kate, smilingly, as she placed the jewels carefully in their places, and closed the case. These were the kind of replies that her husband had to be content with, in the moments when he longed for some affectionate look or word; and they made him reflect and wonder if Kate did care at all for him, and if not, why had she married him? She must have had, in fact he knew she had, plenty of handsome younger men, who had paid her marked attention, and would have thought themselves fortunate to claim her as a wife; so that after all she must have cared for him more than any of these at least. Then some women, he knew, never made any demonstration of their feelings;

and perhaps Kate was one of those, he thought, who did not, so he must conquer these mean jealous feelings, and love her just as she was, and be content to make the best of things.

They were welcomed at Charing Cross by Mr. Byrne and Miss Casteldi. Kate saw her father instantly, and rushed into his arms, " so glad to see his dear face again," she said.

" Why, my precious Kitty, welcome back again. How well you look, love! Continental life and dissipation have suited you wonderfully. Ah, Denton," he exclaimed, as he came up to him, " glad to get you here again. I was telling Kate how hearty she looks, and what good care you must have taken of her."

" Then, papa, you are quite mistaken, for we have had no dissipation of any kind; at least, I have not. We were only saying as we came along this afternoon how quiet we have been," said Kate. " But I intend to make up for it now, papa, as you are here

and dear Aunt Neta. George has so much
to do, he says, so he can do it without
thinking of us."

" You ungrateful girl to say such things,"
said her father, laughing. " Why, Denton
has spoiled you already, I see."

They drove to Farrance's, where they
dined, and intended to stay a day or so,
as Lord Denton wanted to see the house
they had empowered his agent to take for
them before they went into it. It proved
quite satisfactory and comfortable, was
handsomely furnished, and nicely situated,
overlooking Hyde Park and Kensington
Gardens. They had taken it only for the
season, thinking they would not take one
of their own, as, of course, if anything
happened to the sickly heir, they would
have a very large one, with the title and
estate.

Kate entered into all the gaieties of the
London season with great enjoyment, every-

thing was so new and fresh to her. The
garden parties, opera, concerts, and balls,
which came so rapidly, were most of them
honoured with her fair presence. She was
undoubtedly the most lovely woman of any
assembly. Her charming voice was an
additional cause of her being admired and
courted, and made her a great favourite
with almost all her new circle of friends.
She was presented by the Countess of
D——, an old acquaintance of her husband's family; and surely our Most Gracious
Majesty never received homage from a more
beautiful subject. The waiting in the Park
had made Kate quite impatient, and she
wondered how any one could attend a
drawing-room without great fatigue and
losing their temper. " Do pull that blind
down, please," she said to the Countess.
" Look at that horrid man staring at us ;
how can you bear it ? "

" My dear Lady Denton, you must get

used to this. We are here to be looked at, my dear; and if I had pulled the blind down in that man's face, he would, I dare say, have shouted at us, and caused a *fracas* with the police. Poor things! they come quite close sometimes, just to have a good peep at our jewels. They don't see such as yours every day, you know."

"I am sure this waiting might be avoided; at least, one would think so. There is exactly half-an-hour till we begin to set down, you say?" asked Kate.

"Yes, dear; but it is a lovely day, which is not so unpleasant as a raw, cold one would be. The last drawing-room day was quite like winter. I pitied my poor coachman and footmen more than myself. But take my advice, and bring a book or some crochet whenever you are alone; it helps the time over. I know several women who do so: you don't notice the outsiders quite so much."

Kate found that the waiting was not the only annoyance she met with that day She had to force her way through a crowd of satin, lace, and tulle trains and flounces to the Throne-room, where she arrived with heightened colour, which enhanced the beauty of her youthful face, and called forth many remarks and suggestions as to the genuineness of her complexion.

Before the season was more than half over, the weather set in very hot, and Mr. Byrne began to tire of the continuous bustle of a London life. Kate never seemed to care to go anywhere without him; and, of course, so long as he felt equal to it, it was a great pleasure to him. But he found that the irregularity caused sleeplessness and loss of appetite, so he spoke of returning to Ireland with Aunt Neta. But Kate was so averse to their leaving, and pleaded so hard for them to stay a little longer, that he found it almost impossible not to give way to her.

"Don't go, please, papa; I shall be so lonely without you; I shall, indeed. There's no real necessity to go yet. Aunt, you try to persuade him, do," Kate said, turning to Miss Casteldi, and looking eagerly at her.

"Lonely? Nonsense, Kitty; you have your husband and more friends than I can count. That's a great mistake of yours, my dear," replied her father.

"And," said Aunt Neta, "your papa is not resting well just now, Kate, love, and wants more quiet; besides, the heat is very trying to old people."

"Yes, Kate," replied her father, "all this racketing about does knock me up terribly. I am not so young as I used to be, you see."

"Well, but, papa, you can rest here as much as you like. I won't ask you to go to a single place with me if you do not care for it,—I will not, indeed; and as to the heat, why, it will be quite as bad at · home as it is here," said Kate.

"Oh, yes, I know that, my dear; but when one is not just the thing, there is no place like home. So I think you must make up your mind to spare us, Kate, in a day or two, as I have some pressing business matters to attend to, and I cannot very well see to them here."

"I am really and truly sorry, papa, but of course, if you want to go for your health's sake, I ought not to try to dissuade you. Nor can I ask Aunt Neta to stay if you go, because you can't do without her, I know; but I shall miss you both so much. I hate partings above all things," said Kate.

While the conversation had been going on, Lord Denton sat sipping his wine, and taking no part in it. He thought it very hard to have to sit at his table and hear his wife beg for company to stay with her, when for the last two months or more he had scarcely seen her alone, except at rare intervals, for a few minutes. As far as he was concerned, he would be very glad to have his house free for a little. The constant coming and going had not been altogether to his taste, nor added to his comfort, in many senses of the word. So when Kate did ask him if he thought papa need go away, he said that "he thought Mr. Byrne had looked bored for a long time, and that it was the very best thing he could do."

CHAPTER XI.

"OTHING lasts for ever," some one says, which is very true. Kate had to say good-bye to her father and aunt, and the London season came to a close. Every day the fair and fashionable residents were fewer and fewer, till at last most of the large grand houses were closed and tenantless, and the parks and squares had that dry, dusty, faded appearance which comes in with the dog-days. Still the Dentons lingered, not that they, either of them, particularly cared to do so, but because they were waiting to know when Helen Leigh would be able to join them for a jaunt to the Highlands.

Kate had tried to persuade Mrs. Leigh to allow Helen to pay her a visit in London, but for some reasons, known only to themselves, they declined all the kind offers for a little fashionable life. When Kate consented to go to the North, she instantly thought of Helen, and wrote at once to ask her to join them, and begged for a quick reply. As one did not come by return of post, she became impatient, and begged Lord Denton to write too. This rather surprised him, for he had been anticipating their making this outing together; not that he had any objection to Miss Leigh,—on the contrary, he thought her a very nice girl, and had received so much kindness from her mother, that he could not possibly raise any objections to his wife's plans.

" I want to give Helen the treat, George," she said. " We used to say we should like to see Scotland together. You like her very much, I know ; don't you, now ? And con-

sider how many months it is since I saw the
dear thing. I would almost rather not go
if she does not come, but go straight to
Denton from here."

The result of this was that his Lordship
wrote, and begged Mrs. Leigh to give them
both the pleasure of her daughter's company, and promised to take every care of
her if she would spare her. Helen followed
her mother's acceptance very soon, and they
at once started for Edinburgh. The two
friends found plenty to talk about. Kate
was full of past pleasures and future plans,
and showed wonderful interest in all news
Helen had to tell of her quiet life.

"I intend to do great things this winter,
Nellie, I assure you. I won't promise faith-
fully to teach and preach as you do, but
I mean to be somewhat interested in my
husband's tenants, and become the Lady
Bountiful, as, I suppose, I shall be expected
to be."

"A move in the right direction, dear Kate. This is a most cheering surprise, indeed. You, who a year ago despised the idea of being interested in poor people, and scolded me for being so into the bargain."

"Now that is what I call very spiteful for you, Nellie. When one wishes to reform, she should not have her past misdeeds thrown out to her. What is done and gone can't be remedied anyhow, but an improvement may take place in the future. I say ' may ' advisedly, for all my castles may tumble down to mere nothings; but I suppose to be perfectly proper I must appear interested, even if I really am not."

"My dear Kate, I was quite in fun, I assure you, and of course you will do everything that you have thought of. Circumstances alter cases. You did not think of becoming Lady Denton when we last talked about these things."

Helen wrote long accounts home of their

journeyings, giving to her mother minute details of all the beauties of the western coast. She was most enthusiastic in her admiration of all the places they had visited, especially the queen of lakes, Glencoe, and Staffa.

"While we were at Tarbet, mamma," she wrote, "we went across the lake in a tiny boat to Rowerdennen. We could have gone by the steamer, but Kate wished for a row, and the lake was as smooth as glass, so, though I was dreadfully frightened at the bare idea, I put a good face on the matter, and got in, really enjoying the row across, it was so very calm. But we had scarcely started back again, when it became furious, and we were tossed about terribly. Such waves, mamma; you can scarcely imagine how angry they were. I was quite ill with fear and trembling, and gave vent to my misery with sundry groans, much to the amusement of Kate, who actually sat and enjoyed the wetting. Lord Denton assured me there was no danger, although he looked anxious; but I could take no comfort from anything he said, and appealed every now and then to the Highland lads who were rowing us. Thankful was I, dear mother, to place my feet once again on the land, and there is no doubt that we had a narrow escape; and I have assured Kate that nothing shall ever induce me to put a foot into a nutshell of a boat again to risk my precious life in that way. There were some pretty little children on Iona, selling small green stones in saucers. One of them, a little girl, took my fancy immensely. I spoke to her, and kissed her tiny brown hand, which surprised her and her companions a good deal. Everywhere we go, both in towns and villages, we find the children barefooted. They fly along, escaping wonderfully the bits of stone and things, which one expects would hurt them very much indeed.

I longed to be able to shoe them all, but I found that if I could have done so, I should get no thanks for my pains, nor would boots be acceptable to many of them. The hotels and steamers are full of Americans, who seem to be rushing through this beautiful land with great speed.

"It is so enjoyable, travelling as we do, mamma,—not a thought or care. Lord Denton manages everything easily. Sends here and there for rooms, which are always ready for us. Kate has her own way in everything, as you may suppose, and he evidently takes great pleasure in obeying her every wish and fancy, and she has no fewer than before her marriage, mamma, I assure you. We talk a good deal of you, love, and Kate hopes to see us very often when they return, and settle for the winter at the Court, which will now be very soon, as they are coming with me as soon as a large ball is over which we are all going to, and it is to be on a grand scale. Inverness is very full, and there is plenty of gaiety going on everywhere, as it happens to be the festive season."

There were great preparations for the return of Lord Denton and his bride. The house was quite finished, and only waited for its master and mistress coming home. The volunteers met them with their band at the station, and they drove to the Court through many arches of evergreens, flags, and flowers, with any number of "Welcomes" all along the route. A good many people were waiting in the roads to catch sight of Lady Denton, who put on her sunniest smiles and most gracious bows on all sides, winning the hearts of those she bestowed them on.

"Ah, things will be different now," they said. "My Lady will be sure to stay at the Court, and make a little life about the old place."

Of course the men had to be feasted, and

Lord Denton made a little speech, which must have given great satisfaction, if one could judge from the hearty cheer which followed.

"Well, Kitty, are you pleased with your reception to your new home?" said Denton, as he entered the drawing-room, where he found Kate reading letters.

"Oh, yes; quite delighted," replied Kate, getting up, and going to the window. "And what handsome rooms these are! I have looked in everywhere, and seen everything already. My rooms are simply perfection, and this look-out I like so much too. I am glad my own room looks this way. You have really been very thoughtful and kind, and I thank you ever so much."

"May you live long to enjoy all these comforts, Kitty, and always be as happy as you are at this moment," replied her husband, as he came to her side.

"Now, don't be sentimental, George, there's a dear, please. I will try my piano after dinner; so come in early, and, if you promise not to fall fast asleep in five minutes, I will sing to you for a treat."

It was one of their jokes, that he always was "soothed over," as he called it, by Kate's voice. She was very annoyed when she noticed that this was usually the result of her singing to him when they were alone, and scolded him for his want of appreciation and rudeness; but he assured her it was a great compliment to her really, for no other voice had ever so charmed him. The truth, perhaps, was that when she did sing to him it was when they had no company, and after dinner, generally soon after; and Lord Denton, like most of his brethren who make a hearty meal of dinner, could not very well resist the inclination for a doze of a few minutes, after which he brightened up considerably.

The first thing Kate did, the next day, was to go and see her friend, Mrs. Leigh.

She drove her husband over in great spirits.

" Dear Mrs. Leigh, I am delighted to see you again. I have so often thought and talked about you, and longed for you sometimes in my quiet moments. What an age it seems since I left this house last, and yet it is very little more than a year ago when I made that never-to-be-forgotten visit," said Kate.

" I am equally glad to see you, dear child," replied Mrs. Leigh, kissing her again, " and must thank you both at once for your kind attention to Nellie. She has enjoyed her visit to Scotland so much, and looks so well, that I cannot thank you enough for thinking of her."

" I was so delighted to have her with us," replied Kate. " Considering all things, we have been singularly fortunate as to weather; for we had very few days when we could not go out at all."

"Yes, so Helen says," replied Mrs. Leigh. "I hope you have come home, Kate, with a turn for quiet life, and intend to give yourselves a thorough rest. I am sure you are sadly in want of it."

"Well, I confess I am not sorry to get home," said Lord Denton. "But, as to Kate, nothing tires her. She seems able to bear any amount of fatigue without feeling or showing it in the least. Is it not so, Kate?"

"I really don't know. I am rather younger than some people, I know," replied Kate, laughing; "that may make the difference perhaps: I don't pretend to say. I have told Helen all I mean to do, and she will tell you, Mrs. Leigh, I dare say. Still I don't intend to shut myself out of the world altogether, I must honestly confess; my handsome house will want guests, and I hope to fill it often."

"There are many reasons, Kate, for you

to take care of yourself now," replied Mrs. Leigh; "but I shall come and have a long chat with you in a day or two, and talk secrets, as Helen calls my little sermons."

"Thank you so much. I promise to listen attentively, and to become a perfect pattern of goodness. But here comes Nellie, and who is it with her? Why Mr. Clayton, I declare; that is fortunate, as I want to see him too."

When they had been about a fortnight at home, Kate began to make up her list of visitors she intended to ask to come to them.

"I should like to see your list, Kate. I may have some additions to suggest to you," her husband said.

Kate handed him the paper, and watched him as he read it down.

"I think you might add the Laceys and Captain Martin, and Mr. and Mrs. Ponsonby.

'They are all old friends of mine. I should like them to come, if they can, very much."

' "Oh, certainly; the Laceys and Ponsonbys by all means, if you wish, but not Captain Martin, George," replied Kate.

"But why, Kitty? He has always come here; he will think it so odd if he isn't asked. You need scarcely see him; he will be out almost all day. *Why* do you so object to him, Kate? You can surely tell me your reasons."

"No, I cannot. I don't know why myself. I only know that I cannot bear the look of his face; and, unless you wish me to be intensely disagreeable to him and to you too, he will not ever be asked here again, at least when I am here."

"But I am going to write to him just now, Kate; and how absurd and uncivil it will seem not to tell him to come, especially as he knows almost all of those who are coming. It is quite babyish of you, I must say."

"It may seem so to you. I don't, of course, expect you to understand my feelings; but surely you can make this sacrifice for me, if his not coming amounts to that. You will see plenty of him in town next year, I dare say. Do not bring him here, I beg of you. But," she added, haughtily, "you can, of course, do as you please in your own house without my leave."

"Thank you, Madam," replied her husband, rising, and looking very angry. "When I wish for any friends again I shall not trouble you or your crotchets."

He left the room as he spoke, and perhaps it was as well that he did; for his tone of voice and manner were so different from anything she had ever seen or heard from him, she could scarcely believe it was her lord and master, who usually was so good-tempered and kind. But, instead of angering her, it made her feel an irresistible desire to laugh. His attempt to mimic her haughtiness became him so ill, that it amused her immensely, and she indulged her merriment at his expense.

In consequence of the above conversation, Lord Denton wrote to Captain Martin, asking him to let him know where he was, and what he was going to do with himself, and if he had made any plans. His Lordship thought this the wisest thing to do, as it was just possible Martin might have accepted some other invitation; he had plenty of friends who were always glad to get him to join any bachelor parties, he was such capital company. He determined not to say a word to Kate about what he said to his friend. He had regained his temper almost as soon as he left her, and when they met again they both appeared as if nothing had happened to disturb or annoy them. No reply came for some days to this; every post Lord Denton expected and hoped for one, only to be disappointed. He thought he would run up to

town, to make inquiries; then he altered his
mind, and waited, and was rewarded, "after
many days," by getting a foreign letter in
the well-known handwriting, dated from Nice,
where Captain Martin had to take up his
residence for another winter.

"I am quite an invalid," he wrote; "my
cough worse than ever; and I suppose I am
doing the best thing I can by staying here
till spring, by which time I hope to have
picked up some fragments of my old self,
so as to be able to come to my old haunts
again."

Was ever anything more fortunate for the
Dentons than this? It did away with any
attempt at excuses, and the chance of the
Captain feeling himself neglected or ill-treated
by his old friend. It was a matter of great
surprise to all the Captain's associates that he
managed to keep away from London for so
long. He had so often emphatically declared
to them, that if he was *obliged* to stay out of

town for a few weeks (however charming the
place he had to be in was), he should hang
himself right off; "for," he always added,
"it is the only place I know in the world
that is fit to live in."

It is fortunate both for London and its
inhabitants that all the people of this world
have not the same notions, for it would be
impossible to imagine what dreadful results
would necessarily follow. However, though
he may have contemplated putting his threat
into execution, he never got beyond that,
and managed to live on at Nice in spite of
the dullness he complained so much of. It
may as well be here mentioned, that Captain
Martin did get strong and well again, and
was seen one sunny morning, in early spring
of the following year, "kicking his heels
about town," to use his own expression.
It came to be known afterwards that it was
not only his health that had kept him so
long away. Some person said that the exist-

ence of a certain little place not far from
Nice, which has been mentioned before in a
previous chapter, had been the loadstone,
and that the Captain was unusually flush of
that very necessary article, "money," when
he returned to England after his long absence.

END OF VOL. I.

www.ingramcontent.com/pod-product-compliance
Lightning Source LLC
Chambersburg PA
CBHW020117030726
47498CB00006B/2156